WILD RUSH OF LOVE

Winter Lake

RHIAN CAHILL

Rhian Cahill

Love Me Like You Do
Love The Way You Are
When You Love Someone
Let Me Love You
Wild Rush Of Love

WILD RUSH OF LOVE
WINTER LAKE BOOK 5

Drinks aren't the only thing this barman is serving up.

Tending bar at Winter Lake Lodge, Rush Whelan enjoys all the fun with the female clientele, with none of the commitment. They come for vacation—and for Rush, in his bed—then they go. Until Sabreena. After spending her entire holiday together, Rush still can't get the shy beauty out of his mind. When he finds himself with some unexpected time off, there's only one thing to do—follow Reena home.

Waitress Sabreena Howe is grateful for the built-in family that comes with working at Pat's Pub. Mr. Collins and his brood have taken in more than a few strays, Reena among them. But even with their support, Reena has trouble letting people get close...including Rush. Despite their instant connection, Reena allowed fear to abort what could have been their amazing last night together.

When Rush shows up in Baltimore, Reena finally sets her trepidation aside, exploring her newfound sensuality even though she suspects another brief week together can only lead to heartbreak. Her home is here; Rush's is hundreds of miles away.

But the heart knows no time or distance. If Reena can redefine her definition of home, she'll find love is the greatest wild rush of all.

This is for one of the best women I know, while this isn't the "writing together" we've talked about doing for years, it's close enough.
Love you, Mari

This work has been made possible by a license from Mari Carr. All characters, scenes, events, plots, and related elements appearing in the original Wild Irish series remain the exclusive copyrighted and trademarked property of Mari Carr and her affiliates and assigns and are used herein with the express permission of Mari Carr.

PROLOGUE

RUSH STOOD, white-knuckled fingers gripping the bar, thumbs hooked under the curved timber edge, wondering what the fuck was wrong with him.

He couldn't remember what the hell he was supposed to be doing.

He'd pulled days of double shifts before and never had a problem concentrating on his job in spite of the long, exhausting hours on his feet.

Dammit.

He knew all too well what his problem was, he just didn't want to admit it.

A curvy, five-foot-six-inch package of distraction had him so far off kilter he wasn't sure which way was up anymore. And to top it off, that distraction was no longer here.

He couldn't go for a walk and find her wandering the grounds enjoying the spring sunshine. Wouldn't see her smiling face across the bar late at night.

Like every other guest who came to Winter Lake Lodge, her vacation had ended and she'd gone home.

She'd left, and he hadn't thought to get her fucking phone number.

But he could get it. All he had to do was tap into the lodge's reservation system...

Goddammit.

Scrubbing a hand down his face, he closed his eyes on a growl.

She'd been gone a week—seven days—and unlike every other woman he'd hooked up with over the fifteen years he'd worked at the lodge, he couldn't get this one out of his head.

Sabreena Howe.

She wasn't his type.

He went for older women, ones who'd been around the block a time or two. Ones who knew the score, knew all he offered was a tumble in the sack, mutual pleasure for a night —or the duration of their stay, if they were inclined—but nothing beyond sex. And he'd happily rolled from one bed to the next without a backward glance for years.

Until her.

Reena.

Different from the start with her fresh-faced innocence, smoking-hot body, and a complete lack of pretense, she'd drawn him in. Had him seeking her out when he wasn't working and doing things he'd never done with any woman who'd sought his attention.

He should have known she'd get under his skin.

Christ. She hadn't made the first move, *he* had.

One more thing he'd never done before Reena. *Fuck.* He'd done a shit-ton of stuff that had never been on his radar.

Hiked up to the ridge for a picnic. Rowed a boat to the middle of the lake and floated around under the first rays of the morning sun. Held hands beneath the star-filled sky, talking until dawn peeked over the top of the mountains.

With Reena, it hadn't been about sex.

Sure, he'd wanted in her pants. She was hot. He was male. Only way he wouldn't want in her pants was if he swung the other way, and in the twenty years he'd been indulging in that particular pleasure, he hadn't even *looked* the other way.

They'd spent more time together clothed than not. In fact, he'd only gotten her clothes off once.

The night before she left.

And while there had been the passion and explosive chemistry he had expected, there'd been something different, something...more.

Something he couldn't put his finger on...

She moaned in his ear as he pressed the hard length of his cock against her thigh, her body still shuddering with the orgasm he'd stroked her to.

"Reena," he pleaded with a rock of his hips. "Let me have you."

"Yes..."

Rush wasted no time stripping her of her jeans, stripping his own. His fingers trembled, his limbs shook, need razor sharp as it clawed at his balls. He sheathed his cock, barely keeping it together long enough to roll the latex down and get back between her thighs—

"Hey, Rush."

Snapped from the vivid memory, he jerked, his hips bucking forward, slamming his erection into the metal racks beneath the bar. "Fuck," he grunted, pain ripping through his groin.

"Damn, sorry, didn't mean to startle you." His boss rounded the bar to stand beside him. "Where was your head? I called out twice on my way across the room."

Rush turned his head to face Cam but kept his body

pressed up against the bar. The last thing he needed was for his boss to see where his head had been.

Christ. If the man knew Rush had been screwing around with a guest, he'd probably fire him on the spot.

Cam studied him closely. "You all right?"

He forced a smile. "Yeah. Tired. Been a long week."

"That's what I want to talk to you about. Thanks for doing all the extra hours. What do you think of the new staff?"

"Good. They're good. Competent. Fast learners, and Desi is a wiz with cocktails. I'm thinking we should utilize her skills somehow. Maybe do a specialty cocktail on the weekends. See if we can't draw in more customers."

"Hmm...we could theme them with food or events... Remind me at the next department meeting."

"Sure." Relieved to discover talking with his boss had deflated his cock, Rush moved away from the bar and picked up the clipboard he'd left beside the register before he'd forgotten what he was doing. Again. "I'll have this order on your desk within the hour."

He wasn't on until tonight but with training the five new bartenders over the last week, he hadn't gotten around to placing the liquor order yet and they were getting low on supplies.

The local brews were easy to restock but everything else was trucked in, and they needed to get the order processed today or they wouldn't get a delivery this week.

"Can someone else do that?" Cam asked, reaching for the board. "Me?"

"What? Why?" Rush stared at Cam. Was he worried about overtime? "It'll only take me a few minutes then I'll be out of here."

"I've rearranged the schedule. You're off for the next seven days." Before Rush could form a question, Cam held up a hand and continued, "You're owed holidays, but I'm not taking this time out of your leave. You've worked your ass off for the last week and even when you aren't pulling double shifts, I've noticed you're always working. Take a break. We've got the staff to cover it now and with the reading of Harry's will a week from Monday, we'll be dealing with a new owner—and I'm sure more long hours."

"They're finally reading the will?" God. It had been almost three weeks since Harry's death.

Rush swallowed the lump in his throat that formed every time he thought about the lodge's owner. He still couldn't believe the old guy was gone. They'd been close before Harry had taken a step back to take care of his adopted daughter and granddaughter and hired a GM to run the lodge.

Now he was gone.

"Any idea who Harry left this place to?" Rush asked.

Cam shook his head. "No. But there's plenty of rumor and speculation circulating."

"Usually is around here." Rush frowned, wondering how he'd managed to keep his own liaisons with guests secret over the years when the favorite pastime for locals was gossiping, especially among the staff here at the lodge.

"I remember."

Cam rubbed the back of his neck and Rush noticed the fatigue stamped on his face. It was obvious his boss could do with a few days off too. He opened his mouth to suggest they split the week when Cam sighed, his gaze darting around.

In a low voice, he said, "Listen. I need you fully on deck when the new owner shows up. There's bound to be shit hitting the fan when whoever it is discovers how bad things are around here, and I'm down to only a handful of management and staff I trust."

Rush hadn't been sure what to think of Camden Newell when he'd shown up five weeks ago to take on the general manager position, but the guy had proven he knew what he was doing and wasn't out to run the place into the ground like the previous GM had done for the past four years.

With everything that was going on, it didn't make sense for Rush not to be here though, and it went unsaid that neither of them could guarantee they'd have a job once the new owner showed up.

"Why the hell are you giving me time off? You need me here to cover your back," he argued.

"This is the calm before the storm. Take the time while you can. We'll be working our asses off, or be out on them, once the new owner arrives. I think—no, I *know* we've got things turning around. I want that to continue but that won't happen if I run my best employees into the ground. I'd rather you took some time now. We'll have a few days to get a battle plan together before the will is read and whoever Harry left this place to takes over."

"Are you sure? A few normal work days will have me back up to speed." Hell, if he could clear his head of a certain distracting woman and get a good night's sleep, he'd be back to normal by morning.

Cam waved him off. "No. Not good enough. I've checked your timecards. You never punch in overtime."

Rush shrugged. "I love the job. I'm not here for the money, and living onsite means that's not something I have to worry about."

Besides, he had a trust fund. Not that anyone around here knew about it.

"I don't give a shit whether you need money or not. You

do the job, you get paid or compensated." Cam stepped closer and tugged the clipboard out of Rush's hand. "Take the week off," he snapped in what Rush figured was his do-as-you're-told voice, one Rush hadn't heard from the man until now.

With a grin, he saluted. "Yes, boss."

Cam returned his smile with a muttered, "Smartass."

Rush believed once things settled—if they were both still here—Cam would be someone he'd not only call boss, but friend. They'd already forged a connection and he enjoyed working with someone he respected and trusted. It was a complete turnaround after the last few years.

"Your next shift is Saturday night."

"What about tonight?" Rush frowned. "I've got six 'til close."

"Not anymore. Desi has it covered."

"Oh. Okay. It looks like you have every protest countered."

"I do. Get out of here. Go have some fun and make sure I don't see your face in here unless you're bellied up to the bar for a drink before next weekend," Cam said over his shoulder as he walked into the storeroom at the back of the bar.

Fun? The last time he'd had fun, he wasn't alone.

Rush's mind ticked over. Seven days. He had seven days.

How long would it take to drive to Baltimore? Eight hours?

He glanced at his watch. Seven fifteen. If he got on the road now he could be on Reena's doorstep by tonight. They'd have six days. Another week together.

Fuck.

When had he decided to chase after her?

For seven days, the only thoughts in his head regarding Sabreena Howe were memories. Wishes.

Regrets.

And now he was thinking about hitting the road and driving hours to see her?

To do what, exactly?

CHAPTER 1
THREE WEEKS EARLIER...

REENA CLIMBED out of her rental car and took a deep breath as she pulled on her coat.

God it was cold.

She didn't mind the cold, liked it even, but this, the snap and crack of air so frigid it burned was something else.

Like her clothing, it had layers, snapped frozen in each molecule.

Filling her lungs with another deep breath, she smelled those layers.

Water, snow, forest, damp earth, wood smoke...

It was glorious and she couldn't stop the smile from stretching her mouth wide if her life depended on it.

With a little spring in her step, she headed to the trunk for her bag. She had tried to pack light but how light could you go when you needed all those layers to stay warm? Throw in a two week stay with no inclination to wash and she had ended up with something between light and heavy.

Grinning, she tugged the suitcase out of the car and

dropped it on the gravel driveway. There weren't many cars around the lot, maybe twelve or so, but what was here looked a bit more sturdy than her rental sedan.

Trucks and 4WDs were the order of the day it seemed. Not that it mattered. She had no intention of leaving the Winter Lake Lodge unless it was to hike into the surrounding forest or the twenty minute stroll along the lake edge into town the Lodge's website advertised.

She took one more look at the mountains and lake before dragging her suitcase toward the covered entrance. Maybe she should have pulled up there and dropped her bag off then parked her car.

The drag marks she left in the gravel might have worried her if it wasn't for the fact the coating seemed more gone than not and the dirt beneath, while not wet, was definitely damp and stuck to the wheels of her bag in clumps that flicked up behind her.

When she reached the covered drive she noticed several muddy tracks leading to the wide stairs that told her she wasn't the only one trailing muck. Still, not wanting to ruin the lovely timber flooring she could see at the top of the steps, she used a napkin from her coat pocket to wipe the worst of the dirt off her suitcase wheels.

Satisfied she'd done the best she could given the circumstances, she headed up the stairs to the front doors.

The huge inlaid wood panels that made up the lodge entrance had her stopping a moment to take in their beauty. She wasn't one for art but these were a work of art in her opinion. They had to be handmade. And old. Very, very old.

She raised a hand, wanted to run her fingers over the glossy golden surface and probably would have if one side hadn't opened at that moment to reveal a woman with a welcoming smile.

"Hi, you must be Sabreena. Let me get that bag for you." The woman relieved Reena of her bag before she could get her head around the fact she had called her by name. "Come on in out of the cold. I've got a cup of hot cocoa waiting for you at reception."

"Um, it's Reena. Everyone calls me Reena," she offered as she followed the woman inside. Any attempt to retrieve her bag would be useless because the surprisingly fast woman, who had to be in her fifties, was already at the reception desk by the time she made it inside and closed the door behind her.

Reena took a step and stopped. "Oh."

The foyer opened out to a large area with a two-story stone fireplace that should, from its size alone, overwhelm the room, but didn't. A fire flickered and crackled, the flames low but blazing inside the deep and wide well-used firebox. Drawn to the warmth, she moved closer.

Groupings of comfy looking chairs and sofas in different fabrics and colors, chunky wood tables of various sizes and shapes, filled the space, and what looked like hand-woven rugs were scattered over the dark wood floors.

"It's so beautiful."

"Isn't it? I think it's one of the best features of Winter Lake Lodge. Here." The woman held out a mug of steaming creamy brown liquid. "This will warm you right up. I'm Alice Dean, head of housekeeping. Why don't you take a seat by the fire while I check you in and get your key and welcome pack for you."

"Oh, no, I can—"

"You just relax." Alice patted her arm and steered her toward the fire. "I'll just be a moment then I'll join you."

Reena's chest squeezed, the tone of Alice's request

reminding her of her aunt. Both women knew how to make you do as they asked while couching it as a suggestion.

And really, the armchair near the hearth did look comfy. The brown and cream knitted throw draped over the arm looked soft and snuggly too.

Sighing, she decided the offer of a seat beside a roaring fire and a hot cup of sweet smelling cocoa were too much to resist. Putting her mug on the side table, Reena slipped out of her jacket and placed it on the couch opposite. She picked up her cocoa and, cradling the mug in both hands, lowered herself to the plush armchair and almost passed out with pleasure.

It wasn't just comfy, it was warm and spongy and held her butt and thighs in a perfect caress. Like floating on a cloud, or in a warm bath. Muscles, tight from the long drive, relaxed and Reena allowed herself to sink deeper into the luxuriant seat.

"Ah, yes," Alice murmured as she sat in the chair next to her. "That's so much better. I've been on my feet all morning. It's lovely to take the load off for a few minutes. Need a top-up?" she asked, waving the flask in her hand.

"No. I've barely touched it yet. Too busy admiring my surroundings and sinking into this glorious chair." Bringing the mug to her lips, Reena drew in a deep breath before taking a sip. Sweet and chocolaty with a hint of spice, the warm liquid coated her tongue and flowed down her throat in a warm slide that soothed the slightly raw edge the cold air had given it. "Oh, yeah, that hits the spot."

"It does, doesn't it? We'll just sit here a moment and enjoy the *moment* before we dive into all the information about Winter Lake Lodge, your room, and Winter Lake itself." Alice took a sip from her own mug. "Mmm... Nothing beats Hank's cocoa. I don't know what his secret ingredient is, and

I've tried bribery and blackmail to get it out of him, but I swear, there's nothing like it anywhere in the world. Of course he shared the secret with my niece down at Bake and Brew so I can always get my fix there if he decides to get stingy with it."

"Bake and Brew?"

"Yes, a lovely bakery-cafe down on Lake Front. The info on that is part of your package." She indicated the hand basket on the small table between their chairs. "Carly, my niece, runs it and that child was gifted with the skills to make anything baked or brewed. They do—oh listen to me going on and on, you can find out for yourself when you read through the welcome packet."

"Thank you." Reena peered into the basket. "Are those bath bombs?"

"Yes, they're handmade by one of our locals; you'll find her wellness studio down on Lake Front too. Again, all her information is in there. You'll find a little about all the businesses along the lake as well as activities the Lodge and various Winter Lake companies offer for the region."

"All in there?"

Nodding, Alice said with a grin, "Yep. All in there."

"There's a lot in there." She eyed the half bottle of wine. "Is that a local wine?"

"Oh, no, we don't have a winery. Yet. We've got plenty of local beers and then there's Melt, that shit will knock you on your ass so I'd steer clear of that if I were you. That's a small bottle of one of my favorites out of Napa Valley. It's for when you drop one of those bombs in the clawfoot in your room."

Reena sat up straight. "There's a clawfoot tub in my room?"

"One of the biggest we've got." Alice smiled. "Want to see it?"

"Yes." Reena pushed to her feet. "I might have to drop one of those bombs right now."

"Well, if you do, you'll be able to watch the sun set behind the mountain on the far side of the lake from the tub in an hour or so."

"Sunset? From the tub?" She waved a hand. "Lead the way, Alice. Lead the way to this decadent luxury."

CHAPTER 2

Legs aching, lungs heaving, and heart pounding, Reena pushed on.

She could see it now, the lookout, up ahead through the trees that had started to thin out.

A few more steps...

God, she really didn't want to take them, except she couldn't stop now. Not when she was so close.

She blamed the tub.

It wasn't lack of fitness that had her legs heavy as lead, her lungs burning with each breath, and her heart hammering its way out of her chest. Being a waitress meant she was on her feet all the time, taking thousands of steps a day, while carrying trays loaded with food and drinks and dirty dishes. Plus she walked everywhere. She wasn't a slouch in the exercise department.

It was definitely the tub's fault.

She'd spent three hours in the thing yesterday. Topping up the water to keep it nice and hot every thirty minutes or so until the sun had dropped behind the mountains across the lake and the stars had flickered to life on a blanket of deep blue-black sky.

By the time she'd climbed out and called room service, she was a wrinkly prune and every part of her felt like melted wax, warm and squishy.

Then again maybe it had been the wine she had sipped all afternoon while she watched the day end and the night begin. She probably shouldn't have ordered that second bottle with dinner either.

Yeah, the wine and the tub. They were to blame. They'd made her soft.

They were the reasons for her current struggle to walk up a damn hill.

Okay, fine, not so much of a hill, more like the side of a mountain, but it was a small mountain and it wasn't as though she was going all the way to the top. Nope. She wasn't even going halfway.

She glanced up. Barely twenty feet from the lookout now except from here it seemed like twenty thousand miles.

Everything in her wanted to stop, just stop. Which was why she kept going.

She wasn't a wimp. She'd rest when she got there.

Maybe die a little bit too.

Head down, breath rasping in her ears as a harsh accompaniment to the drumming of her heart, she charged on.

She'd keep going. One foot in front of the other. She *would* make it. One step at a time.

She didn't look up, kept her eyes locked on the hiking boots she'd spent the last six months breaking in, and trudged on, taking those steps one at a time.

The ground leveled off beneath her feet and with her lungs screaming for breath and her legs trembling, she stopped, bent over, and braced her hands on her knees, sucking in air like a damn vacuum cleaner stuck in overdrive.

She just had to catch her breath. Then she'd gloat, revel in the glory of making it to Lake View Lookout.

In a minute.

Maybe.

Oh god.

She really needed to up her game in fitness. Although to give herself some credit, it wasn't like she'd trekked up a mountain before. This was a first and the reason she'd chosen to holiday in Winter Lake. She liked to walk. Loved getting out and walking along the Baltimore harbor. Enjoyed her local parks as well.

Of course those paths didn't weave their way up the side of a mountain where snow still lay in patches on the ground.

They also weren't at twenty-seven hundred feet above sea level.

Maybe she had altitude sickness.

Too out of breath to laugh, Reena choked on the sound before it could form.

Jeez, she *really* needed to up her fitness game.

This didn't bode well for the rest of her holiday.

The plan had been to head up to Fire Trail Ridge but that was three times as long and another five hundred feet up.

She'd have to work her way up to it. That's if she ever managed to make it back to the Lodge. Right now that seemed impossible.

Reasonably sure she'd caught her breath, she eased upright and lost it all over again.

The burst of air that left her lungs sounded like 'wow' but that was debatable.

Water and trees and sky and water and trees and more sky stretched as far as the eye could see.

She took a step closer to the beautiful white draped vista. "It's beautiful. Perfect."

"Yeah, nothing—"

"Argh!" Spinning around, Reena lost her footing and, arms pinwheeling, she flailed about before strong arms wrapped around her middle.

"Easy. I've got you."

She couldn't see who had her, not with her face smushed into a hard shoulder, and when she got her heart out of her throat and back in her chest, her lungs breathing normally, and her legs solid beneath her, she'd worry about that.

Right now whoever had her was the only thing holding her upright.

"Here, sit." He managed to move her a few feet and park her butt on what appeared to be a naturally formed rock bench. He crouched in front of her, holding out a bottle of water. "Take a sip."

"Thanks." She sucked in a breath, waved his offer aside. "I have my own."

Her gloves made it hard to get the small drink bottle out of her pocket and she wasn't surprised to hear the small huff of exasperation from her would-be rescuer as he brushed her fumbling hands aside and took over.

When he popped the lid and held it out she muttered 'thanks' again before taking it in both hands and slugging back a few big gulps.

"All good now?"

"Yeah." Reena sighed. "Sorry about that. You scared the crap out of me."

"Didn't mean to. I thought you saw me." His smile kicked up higher on the left side and his blue eyes rivaled the sky above them. "You stopped right next to me."

"I did?" She'd been too busy trying to catch her breath.

From the trek up here and then the mountains and lake... She pointed at the view behind him. "Guess I was a little distracted."

He turned to look over his shoulder. "Yeah, it just grabs you and holds on, doesn't it? You never get used to it."

It wasn't the only thing grabbing her. Now that she'd gotten a little more oxygen to her brain, she was noticing more than the gorgeous view. The man crouched before her was gorgeous too. And all man.

He looked like a lumberjack.

Well, what Reena imagined one would look like. Jeans, flannel shirt, thick muscles filling out both, dark scruff covering a strong jaw, that lopsided smile, and those sparkling blue eyes combined to make one hell of a view in her opinion.

"So." He turned back, held out a hand. "Rush."

"What?" She took his hand. "Rush?"

He grinned. "My name. Rush. Rush Whelan."

"Oh! Reena. Sabreena Howe." She returned his grin with one of her own. "Nice to meet you, Rush. Is that a nickname?"

"Nope, it's what's on my driver's license." He grinned.

CHAPTER 3

After a day of lying around—in bed and in the scandalously decadent tub—Reena finally managed to pull on some clothes and headed out of her room.

She'd woken this morning with so many aches and pains she'd barely—and yes, she'd crawled—made it out of bed to use the bathroom.

Pain meds and room service had been the order of the day. And when the meds eased some of the discomfort she'd hobbled back to the bathroom and filled the tub with water so hot her skin was still pink.

But it worked. It had taken the better part of the day and three different sessions soaking in the tub but finally, *finally*, she could walk without looking like she'd broken every bone in her body. Or whimpering in pain.

She wasn't up for a walk into town but she was able to make her way downstairs to the Bar and Grill, the Lodge's onsite restaurant and bar.

The place was quiet when she walked through the wide wooden archway. A couple sat at a table in one corner, two men—not together—sat on stools at the bar. She was debating where to sit when a woman in black pants and white shirt beneath a red apron headed toward her.

"Good evening. Table for one?"

Smiling, Reena nodded.

"Right this way."

Following, she scanned the room. Lots of wood and a smaller rock fireplace similar in style, and she was sure built from the same stone, as the one in the Lodge's main room held her gaze as they stopped beside a two-seater on the other side of the space.

"Oh, would you like to sit by the fire?"

"Can I? I love the one in the main room."

"You could eat out there if you want; we serve there too."

"No, that's all right. If I can have one of the tables close to this one that would be great."

"Sure." The woman made quick work of getting her settled by the fireplace and taking her drink order. "I'll be back with your hot cocoa."

Reena had decided to stay clear of wine tonight. She hadn't had any since her first night and with the pain meds she'd been popping like candy all day she figured it would be best not to partake again yet.

"Hey! Reena."

Glancing over at the bar she found her gaze caught by a bright blue one. The smile overtook her face as she whispered, "Rush."

"Kennedy get your drink order?" he asked as he came out from behind the long wood-topped bar and moved toward her.

"Yes. Yes, she did. I ordered a mug of the house hot cocoa."

"Good choice." He pulled out the chair next to her and

sat. "So, kind of strange that we spent a couple of hours together yesterday and neither of us mentioned this place."

"Yeah." She shrugged. "It didn't really come up."

"No. Well, I work here. Manage the bar. Live here too. In the staff quarters."

She smiled. "And I'm staying here for two weeks."

He nodded at the menu in front of her. "Planning on dinner?"

"Yes. Seeing how you work here, what would you recommend?" She closed the menu and folded her hands on top of it.

"That depends what you're in the mood for." He leaned closer. "Want some company? I just finished my shift and was going to grab something in town but I'd rather sit here with you if that's an option."

"Yes. Of course. Definitely." She handed him the menu. "And that means you're in charge of ordering dinner."

She'd enjoyed the time she'd spent with Rush yesterday. They'd hung out at the lookout for about an hour. He'd pointed out landmarks, buildings they could see down in Winter Lake and where other lookouts were around the lake as well as a general overview of the town and surrounding area before they had walked back down to the parking lot.

And she had to admit she'd been a little sad when they'd said goodbye, gotten into their own vehicles and gone their separate ways.

Now he was here.

"Good. I'll go put our order in and grab a drink. Back in a sec." He tucked the menu under his arm and pushed to his feet. Waving at the waitress who'd seated Reena, he called out, "Don't worry, Kennedy. I've got this."

Kennedy looked between them with a questioning glance but didn't say anything. She placed a thick white mug filled to the brim with the creamy brown liquid Reena knew was smooth as silk on the table and said, "I'll leave you in Rush's capable hands."

She was gone before Reena could say thank you. Looking around, she saw the couple from the corner was gone and one of the men at the bar had also left. The fire crackled merrily a few feet away, the warmth surrounding her along with the scent of wood.

She'd loved the main room, and her own room, but she thought this room might actually be her favorite. There was an intimacy here that was missing in the big room, and while her room with its king size bed and huge tub was intimate due to the fact it was a bedroom and private, this room, the long bar, the stools, the tables and chairs...there was something sexy about it.

Her gaze found Rush as he came through a side door.

Then again maybe it felt sexy because of the man walking toward her with that lopsided smile and sparkling blue eyes.

He walked with a swagger but it didn't appear forced. It was a natural roll of his hips resulting from those thick-muscled legs eating up the ground between them.

He placed a mug of beer on the table and retook his seat. "So. Tell me all there is to know about Reena."

"What do you want to know?" She took a sip of her drink. "Oh, god. This is the best thing I've ever tasted."

Rush grinned. "It's the special ingredient."

"So I'm told." She took another sip then put her mug down. "Okay, about Reena. I'm twenty-five, live in Baltimore, work in a family owned Irish pub with an attached restaurant. That's pretty much it."

"Siblings?"

"No. Only child."

"Ditto. And I've got ten years on you. I've been here, at

the Lodge, for fifteen years, the last ten as Bar and Grill's manager."

"Do you like it? Managing the bar?"

"I did. I didn't. And now I do again."

"Oh?"

He waved that away. "Long story. Not really dinner conversation. Okay, so tell me the plan."

"What plan?"

"For your holiday. You strike me as the type to have a plan."

"Actually I'm not. Usually. But you're right. I've got a plan for the next two weeks. Although yesterday may have put an end to that." Reena frowned.

"Why?"

"Well, as embarrassing as it is to admit, and even more so to know you saw, I barely made it up to the lookout and I wanted to go up to Fire Trail Ridge while I was here." Sighing she added, "There's no way I'll make it all the way up there without dying."

Rush chuckled. "You're not used to the altitude. It won't take much to get you there. Why don't I take you on some of the easier treks around here, then when you're ready we can hit Hargrove Trail up to Fire Trail Ridge."

"Oh, I couldn't ask you to do that."

"Why not? I like hiking and I usually do some in my free time anyway, so why wouldn't I want to do it with a pretty woman at my side?"

Warmth filled Reena's face. She wasn't used to men calling her pretty. She'd never been one of those women who men hit on.

Not that Rush's comment was a line; she could tell he meant what he said and while she might be a little uncomfortable with the attention, it was a pleasant sensation that was unfamiliar rather than embarrassing or disturbing.

And really, was she going to knock back his offer to show her the area? He'd lived here for over a decade—he would know all the best places to see.

"Are you sure?" she asked and took another sip of her delicious cocoa.

Nodding, he reached for his beer. "I'd love to spend some time showing you Winter Lake."

"Deal." She stuck out her hand. When his warm hand enveloped hers, she sucked in a breath.

She hadn't planned on a holiday romance no matter what her friend Caitlyn had been saying ever since Reena had booked this trip, but if she were honest, Rush made her think about it.

CHAPTER 4

RUSH FILLED the below-bar fridge with more bottles of beer with a smile on his face. Yes, he loved his job and it made him happy to be doing something he loved but that wasn't why he was smiling.

Nope. The no doubt goofy grin on his face was because of Reena.

He'd taken her along the edge of the lake to a small secluded clearing to the west of the Lodge on their first hike. He'd only had a few hours before he had to start work but they'd gotten in a good walk and she seemed to handle it well. Unlike Sunday when she'd been all but breathless up on Lake View Lookout.

She'd even managed to carry on a conversation while they dodged trees and the mounds of snow that still stuck to the ground.

The weather was warming up, and there wasn't any snow in the forecast but it was still cold. Still required layers for venturing out longer than a few minutes.

He'd enjoyed showing her some of the place he'd called home for the last fifteen years.

Couldn't wait to show her more.

He figured he'd take her along Lake Front tomorrow, let her explore the shops that lined the street, before he started his night shift. He glanced at his watch. Four. They'd been apart only five hours and already he was thinking about when he'd see her next. Hell, he'd been thinking about it the minute he'd left her outside the door to her room.

Tuesdays were slow—then again most days were in recent years—so they only needed three bar staff for the whole day. He had the mid-shift today. Luke had opened and Desi would close. They had seen a steady increase in business since Cam had taken over as GM—since Harry had come out of retirement to take a more active role in the day-to-day running of the Lodge.

Rush had been ready to confront Harry about what was going on at the Lodge when the last GM had disappeared.

No one knew why he'd gone or where he'd gone and, as far as Rush was concerned, good riddance. He was glad they'd seen the last of Lawrence George Farnham. He'd been an asshole as well as a pompous prick and couldn't manage a business out of a wet paper bag.

With Cam in the GM role and Harry back on deck, things were going to improve. They had improved. And he knew it was only the beginning. Things would soon be back to those heady days of standing room only and nonstop work.

"Rush."

His head snapped up. Cam stood in the entry to the bar. The look on the man's face was enough to have Rush's insides cramping, a heavy weight filling his chest. Whatever put that look on Cam's face wasn't good. He didn't need words to know the world was about to shift.

Slowly he pushed upright, walked around the end of the bar.

"Harry's dead."

"What?" He stumbled. "Dead? How?"

"Accident. On the road in from the highway." Cam placed a hand on the archway. "I... I just..." He shook his head. "Matilda. Lark."

"But..." Rush glanced at the seat Harry had sat in yesterday afternoon. He'd come in to talk to Rush about the bar. About how they could pull in more customers. Not just those who stayed at the Lodge but locals. "He was just..."

"Kennedy called." Cam staggered toward a seat, sank into it. "She was at Larissa's House, with Jagger. Ren told her."

"Jesus." Rush dropped into a chair beside Cam. "I can't... When?"

"Last night I think. Kennedy wasn't sure. She and Ren are going over to Harry's now. To see Lark. She'll call me after she knows more." He looked around the room. "I gave her the night off. I'll work if you need waitstaff."

Rush shook his head. "I doubt we'll need it." He leaned over; resting his elbows on his knees, he cradled his head in his hands. "Fuck. Harry."

"I know." Cam pushed to his feet. "I need to find Alice. I don't know what to do about the rest of the staff."

"I'll tell Hank. Desi when she comes in. Jesus, Cam. What the fuck will happen with the Lodge?"

"I don't know. Other than Matilda and Lark, and Ren, Harry doesn't have any family." He placed a hand on Rush's shoulder. "Call if you need me to come back."

"Yeah, okay."

When Cam left, Rush sat trying to get his head around Harry being dead. It didn't seem real but it had to be. He needed to go to the kitchen, tell Hank. The chef, like Rush and Alice, had been at the Lodge for years, had been friends with Harry as well as an employee.

Jesus, did Burt know? Rush hadn't seen him today but Burt and Harry went back far longer than anyone else around here; they'd grown up together.

Detouring behind the bar, Rush grabbed a bottle of Harry's favorite Macallan and two shot glasses. They'd need a splash to get them through this.

The big guy was at the stove stirring a big pot of what smelled like his famous beef stew. Over the years Rush had devoured many a bowl of Hank's beef stew.

"Hey." He put the glasses on the counter and cracked the bottle. Filling each glass to the rim he took a moment to cap the bottle and put it down. Blowing out a breath he said, "There ain't no easy way to say this so I'll just get it out there. Harry's dead. Car accident. I don't know details. Kennedy called Cam, Cam told me. Just now."

He picked up the glass and held it out. Hank stared at him for a full minute before he walked over and picked up the other glass.

"Harry," Rush murmured as he tapped his glass to Hank's and sank the shot.

After a quiet moment Hank asked, "We got anyone out there?"

Rush shook his head.

"Maybe we should shut up for the night. It's not like we get many in on a Tuesday."

"Yeah, maybe we can take this bottle back into the bar and call Cam and Alice down."

Hank nodded. "I'll just..." He looked around. "Yeah, okay, let's call Cam and Alice down."

Rush picked up the bottle and his glass, left the other for Hank to bring out, and went back to the bar. He dragged a stool out and sank onto it. "Fuck."

He didn't know how long he sat there before Hank sat beside him, before Cam came in with his arm around a quietly crying Alice and Rush moved to a table, took the bottle, two extra shot glasses, and his own.

Nobody spoke as he poured. Alice's sniffles were the only sound until they each picked up a glass and held it out.

Hank drew in a breath. "He'd want this place to keep going."

"Yes, he would," Alice agreed.

"I'll do what I can, but I guess it's up to whoever he left this place to," Cam said.

"Wouldn't that be Matilda? Maybe Lark or Ren? He thought of the two of them as family," Hank offered.

Cam shook his head. "I don't know. He never talked about it. Why would he?"

"To one of the best men I ever knew," Alice said and tapped her glass against everyone else's. "Harry."

"Harry," they chorused.

CHAPTER 5

SHE HADN'T MEANT to listen but by the time she realized what Alice and the other man were talking about it was too late to sneak away. So instead, she'd slunk lower into the chair and hoped neither of them noticed her.

When they left the foyer, the man had slipped his arm around Alice's shoulder and led her into the Bar and Grill. Reena breathed out the breath she'd held and eased up in the seat.

Rush had talked about Harry on their hike earlier today. She knew he'd be upset and she wanted to find him, offer comfort, but didn't know if it was her place. They'd only met two days ago and while she thought they were developing a friendship, did it reach deep enough for her to offer solace?

She knew what it was like to lose someone unexpectedly. When Aunt Beth had a stroke and died, Reena's whole world had shifted and when the shaking had stopped, nothing had been the same.

Without her job—the Collins family—she didn't think she'd have been able to get through those first few weeks.

The front door banged open behind her, making her jump. Spinning around she watched a man in a suit, a scowl on his face, stalk to the reception desk, around it, and through the door behind.

She knew that led to the offices but she was pretty sure, from Rush's earlier descriptions that the General Manager had been the man with Alice.

And they'd gone into the Bar and Grill.

Standing, she'd taken two steps toward the restaurant entrance when the man burst back into the foyer.

"No wonder this place has gone to shit. Where the fuck is everyone?"

"Can I help you," Reena asked, straightening her spine and moving toward the clearly angry man.

"Who the hell are you?"

"Reena. Can I help you...?"

"Yes. Where's your boss, the General Manager?"

She didn't bother to correct his assumption she was an employee and not a guest; this guy clearly had no clue and wouldn't care anyway. "I'll get him for you. Who can I say is asking?"

"Sturgis, Jeremy Sturgis. I'm Harry Windburn's lawyer."

Reena dipped her chin in acknowledgment and headed to the restaurant.

They were sitting around a four-top close to the bar when she walked in. They looked so lost and she hated to interrupt but...

She glanced over her shoulder, thankful to find the lawyer hadn't followed her.

"Excuse me."

"Oh. Reena!" Alice jumped to her feet. "I'm sorry—"

"No, sit." She raced over, eased Alice back into her chair

then faced the man she assumed was the General Manager. "Cam?"

"Yes," he said as he slid his chair back and stood.

"There's a man in the foyer. Said he's Harry's lawyer. Jeremy Sturgis."

"Shit." Cam spun on his heel. "I'll deal with him."

"Hey." Rush put his hand on hers. "You okay?"

"Me?" She looked down at him, could see the sorrow swirling in his eyes. "I should be asking all of you that. Can I do anything?"

Alice sighed. "Reena is our only guest tonight. I think it best if we just close up and start again in the morning. Hank? Rush?"

"Yeah," the big guy Reena guessed was Hank stood. "I'll leave the stew on the stove if anyone wants it but I'm going to head out."

Rush's fingers squeezed hers. "Want to have a bowl of stew with me? I can guarantee you haven't tasted anything like it."

"Sure. Do you need help closing down?"

"Damn. I need to call Desi, let her know not to come in."

"She's probably already on her way. She's staying over in Broken Bay." Alice glanced at her watch. "I'll wait and let her know when she gets here."

"Are you sure?" Rush asked.

"Yes. I'll call Alex while I wait."

"I'll bring you a bowl before I go, Alice." Hank nodded at Rush then headed through the side door.

"Why don't we bundle up and eat out on the dock?" Reena suggested. "It's a beautiful clear night out there." She remembered sitting outside—in the dark—for hours after her aunt died. Something about the stars, the vastness of the universe, had helped her come to terms with her loss.

"Okay. I'll get the stew, you grab your jacket and a couple of the blankets from the main room."

By the time they made it outside, Reena had decided on how she wanted to direct their conversation.

"So," she said as she settled into one of the chairs Rush had dragged out on to the dock. "Tell me about Harry."

"He's the most amazing man I've ever met."

"Oh?"

"He's never met a soul he didn't know how to help even when they didn't know they needed helping." She could hear the grin in his voice. "He took a chance on me when I first got here. I wasn't old enough to work in the bar but I had a fake ID that he just arched an eyebrow at and gave me the job."

"Trusting."

"Oh no, I've seen him walk people out or shut them down. He has the uncanny ability to judge you in a split second."

"You love him."

Rush laughed. "Yeah, I guess I do. He's the closest thing to a father I've ever had. My own couldn't give a shit about me, which is how I ended up here in the first place."

"You'll miss him."

"He'd stepped back from the Lodge in recent years so we haven't been as close as we once were, but yes, he'll be missed. The whole of Winter Lake will miss him. He's the mayor and he has all these community projects that help out the town, its people. He's always been a driving force, involved in everything in one way or another. I'm not sure what will happen now." He leaned over and put his bowl on the dock beneath his chair, the stew untouched. "I don't think I'm going to be good company tonight."

"That's okay. I don't mind the quiet."

Reena placed her own bowl down then tipped her head back to look up at the twinkling sky.

Reaching over she grabbed Rush's hand and weaved their fingers together as best she could with them both wearing gloves.

He didn't protest and she took that to mean he was happy for her to stay. If he asked her to leave him alone, she would. But she remembered the dark, the ache that filled the chest, and she knew he'd find comfort in just having her close.

They didn't have to talk. She didn't need entertaining and he didn't need idle chatter.

With the stars brightening above them and the night growing darker around them, she listened to the sounds of the forest, of ice cracking on the lake, of life, and remembered what it was like to need the peace.

CHAPTER 6

"You ready?"

"No."

Rush laughed. "Yes, you are. Come on. There's a reward when we get up there."

"What kind of reward?" Reena asked as she settled her backpack on her shoulders.

"Might be chocolate." He grinned.

"Hank's?" She followed him as he walked backward away from his truck.

"You'll have to get to the top to find out." He reached out a hand. "Let's do this."

"You sure I'm ready for this?"

"Reena." He squeezed her hand when it slid into his. "You can do this."

She blew out a breath. "You'll carry me if I can't?"

Laughing, he turned around and tugged her onto the trail. "I won't need to."

He wouldn't. They had spent every free moment in the last two weeks hiking in and around Winter Lake. He'd even convinced her to take a boat out on the lake early one morning. That had taken some fast talking but he'd finally convinced her the sheets of ice still covering the lake in places weren't going to sink them like the Titanic.

"Have I steered you wrong so far?" he asked as he picked up the pace. He wanted to get there before the sun hit its peak. Plus if need be, they could take their time coming down after their picnic.

"No. In fact you seem to know what I'm capable of better than me," she grumbled.

Swinging their joined hands between them he asked, "You ready to head home?"

She glanced at him, the look in her eyes unidentifiable. "No."

"You could extend your stay."

Reena sighed. "I wish I could."

They hadn't talked about what would happen when she left but with her time almost up, Rush couldn't think about anything else. Except he didn't want to end her holiday on a bad note; there had already been enough sadness during her stay, so he'd take their conversation—and minds—in a different direction.

"I know you said taking the boat out on the lake at dawn was your favorite thing so far but I think you're about to discover something that trumps that."

"It's that good up here?"

"Better." He moved in front of her as the trail thinned, his arm twisted behind him so he didn't have to let go of her hand. "Remember how you lost your breath at Lake View Lookout? Well, be prepared for your heart to stop this time."

"I hope you know CPR," she joked.

Rush smiled. "Oh, yeah, I've got you covered." He couldn't wait to kiss her at the top of the ridge.

They'd done a fair amount of making out over the last two weeks. Nothing too heavy. Although he had made it to second base on more than one occasion.

It was funny, he'd never bothered with the lead up to sex before. Sure, he was as good as the next guy at foreplay but it had always been about hitting the home run. With Reena, it was the whole game.

She was heading home tomorrow morning and he hadn't even gotten her naked. And if he were honest, he didn't care. Not that he didn't want to. But he'd enjoyed every minute with her.

She'd helped him through those first dark days after Harry's accident and he had to admit she had a way of turning the aching loss he felt into a positive thing. She'd been quick to point out he'd loved and been loved and that his life, while empty of that connection now, was still full of that love.

Harry would always be a part of him no matter where he went or what he did. Rush would never have realized that without Reena pointing it out.

"Oh, look!"

Her shout snapped him out of his thoughts and, spinning around, he searched the area around them. "What?"

"There." She pointed between the trees. "I can see the lake."

The tension in his body released. He'd never get used to the way she found the smallest thing amazing. He tugged her hand. "C'mon. You'll be able to see the Lodge when we get to the top."

"Really? But we're on the other side of the lake from the Lodge."

"The way the ridge runs, you can see the whole lake. Plus it's the highest point above Winter Lake so you can see everything around it."

"Did you bring binoculars?"

"Sure did."

"How much longer?"

He chuckled. "Is that the adult version of 'are we there yet'?"

"Obviously." She scooted around him, doing the hand tugging this time. "Come on. Hurry up."

"Don't push too hard. We're going higher than you're used to."

"I'm feeling really good and we're already as high as Lake View, right?"

He followed Reena up the trail. "Yeah, about the same now, I think."

"Well then, this is going to be a snap because I'm not feeling it at all. It's like strolling around the mall."

"You still don't want to push it."

"You know this has been one of the best holidays I've ever had and I've done Disney." She looked over her shoulder and winked at him. "Disney's got nothing on Winter Lake."

He bit his tongue. He wanted to say 'then don't go' but he knew he couldn't—shouldn't.

These past two weeks had been a step out of time for both of them.

Would they have connected so deeply without Harry's death?

Rush didn't know. Wasn't sure how to find out.

For now he would concentrate on getting them to the top of Fire Trail Ridge and worry about what happened after tomorrow...well, tomorrow.

CHAPTER 7
ONE WEEK LATER...

Reena's feet barely lifted off the floor as she made her way to the far booth in Pat's Pub. Her feet hurt. Her legs hurt. Her arms hurt. Sinking into the seat, she leaned her head back and closed her eyes with a relieved sigh.

God. Even her damn eyelashes hurt.

"Wow. For someone who recently returned from a two-week vacation, you're looking pretty trashed."

Reena forced one eye open and saw Caitlyn Wallace slide into the other side of the booth. Stretching her lips into a semblance of a smile, Reena hummed. "Hmm...long day."

"Busy next door?" Caitlyn asked, glancing at the archway Reena had shuffled through.

'Next door' referred to Sunday's Side, the restaurant half of Caitlyn's family's business. The place Reena had worked since she was old enough to have a job. A little before that, if you counted the hours she'd hung out while Caitlyn babysat her when Reena had first come to live with her great-aunt Beth in Baltimore.

"Yeah, and we were down a waitress after Felicity took a tumble and rolled her ankle."

Not that Reena's tired state was due to being on her feet carrying trays stacked with food, drinks or dirty dishes for hours on end. But she wasn't about to explain her exhaustion stemmed from seven nights of little sleep. The bliss of slumber had proven elusive since her return from Winter Lake.

"So. How was the trip?" Caitlyn leaned forward, eagerness lighting up her pretty face. "Meet any hunky guys?"

Spine snapping straight, eyes popping wide, Reena stared at her friend and tripped over her own tongue. "W-why do you ask that?"

Caitlyn cocked an eyebrow.

Dammit. She'd given herself away.

She wanted to bang her head on the seat behind her or the table in front, but knew the action would be futile. Knocking herself senseless wouldn't deter her friend. Caitlyn would only sit there and wait until she spilled the beans. She'd been doing that since Reena was eight with a high level of success. Why change things now?

With a sigh, Reena flopped back against the seat. "Fine. I met a guy."

"Do tell," Caitlyn purred. "I want all the juicy details."

"Nothing to tell." There might have been, but...

Well, Reena wasn't sure why she'd stopped Rush. Or why he hadn't kicked her out of his bed when she'd called a halt to their encounter.

"No juicy details," she muttered with self-disgust.

Caitlyn eyed her with curiosity. "Does this guy have a name?"

"Rush."

"What?" Caitlyn blinked, a baffled expression creasing her brow.

Reena smiled. She'd had a similar reaction when Rush had introduced himself. At first she'd thought it was a nickname, but he'd promptly produced his driver's license as proof. "His name is Rush Whelan."

"Unusual name."

"Apparently he was born in half an hour, well before his expected arrival date so his mother called him Rush because he was obviously in one." She shrugged.

It seemed stupid to name a kid that way, but as the days had gone on and she'd gotten to know Rush better, the name fit.

Everything about him was a rush. From the way he looked to the way he moved to the way he made her feel. Then again, he'd taken his time in other ways...

"Did you at least kiss him?" Caitlyn asked. "Please tell me you at least got some tongue action."

Reena laughed. "Yes. There was tongue."

Her friend frowned. "But you didn't do more." It wasn't a question.

She shook her head and once again gave herself a mental kick in the ass.

The orgasm he'd given her before she'd freaked out counted as more, but she wasn't going to mention that mind-blowing event because then she'd have to explain her behavior, and she really didn't want to. Not even to the woman who knew every other detail of her nonexistent sex life.

God. Why had she stopped him?

Caitlyn scrutinized her for a few moments before her frown turned to understanding. "And now you're regretting not taking things further."

"Yes," she sighed. She'd regretted it the second they put

their clothes back on, and hadn't known how to get them back to the place where they would take them off again.

She'd been so stupid, letting her fear stop her from giving herself to Rush. A fool. There hadn't been any man in her twenty-five years who'd inspired such powerful desire. She'd messed around some but never gotten around to going all the way, and now she feared her best chance had passed her by.

"I..." She swallowed with difficulty as words jammed in her throat.

Caitlyn reached for her hand. "It's okay. It wasn't the right time or the right guy."

Reena could only agree on one of those points. "It was the right guy," she whispered.

"Oh, Reena."

Caitlyn slipped out of her side of the booth and squished in next to Reena, wrapping her up in a warm hug, one that brought back memories of childhood and how this woman had become such an important part of her life. The big sister and confidant she'd never had prior to arriving in Baltimore.

"Any chance you'll see him again?" she asked.

A sound that could have been a laugh burst from Reena's throat as she broke her friend's embrace in spite of the overwhelming appeal of staying cocooned in Caitlyn's comforting hug. "Not unless I take another vacation."

"What's stopping you?"

"I... It..."

What *was* stopping her? It wasn't as though she had a job where she was really needed. Finding someone to cover her shifts wouldn't be difficult. More often than not, she was at Sunday's taking orders and delivering food because she couldn't stand to be inside her empty house. Alone. She was pretty sure Caitlyn's family put up with her because they didn't seem to be able to say no to strays.

In the years since she'd met them, the Collins family had treated her like one of their own, welcomed her into their fold with open arms. Except she always felt as though she circled the group rather than mingling among the big, boisterous clan.

"Sabreena. Don't take this the wrong way."

Uh-oh, the use of her full name meant Caitlyn was going to get in her face about her aimless life again.

"You're treading water. Something needs to change. I thought your trip might shake things up."

"It was a holiday, a chance to visit a part of the country I've always wanted to see, not a journey to find myself or change my life." Her words rang hollow though.

Something *had* changed.

Inside, where she'd been happy—content—before her trip, she suddenly itched, twitched and twisted, as though she had to move. Except she didn't know where she was meant to go.

"Why can't you see what the rest of us do?" Caitlyn asked.

"What? What do you see?" She needed someone to tell her.

Since the death of her aunt, Reena had felt like she was floating through life, as though someone had cut the line on her anchor and she was adrift at sea, bobbing around while all the other boats whizzed past on the way to where they were going.

Not that there was anything wrong with having no destination in mind. She was sure plenty of people lived that way.

Why did she need somewhere to go?

She had money, a house, a job she enjoyed, and friends who were like family.

Except...

"Do something with your stories."

Reena jerked away, her mouth dropping open. "They're not mine."

"They are. You wrote them together. *You* illustrated them. Get them published."

She shook her head. "I can't. They're not..." She couldn't imagine letting go of those stories. They were the closest link she had to the woman who'd taken her in, treated her as her own, when no one else wanted her.

"Beth would want you to."

Would she? Reena didn't know. Could never take that step without being sure her aunt would want that—and now it was too late. Still shaking her head, she stammered, "I-I can't."

"Then find something else to do with your talent. Write more stories. Draw the pictures to match."

Reena shook her head so fast her teeth clacked together, her lungs seized, and tears welled in her eyes, stung the back of her nose.

The stories and drawings had always been something she and Aunt Beth did together.

It was something only the two of them shared.

They were never meant for anyone else, and she couldn't imagine doing a story without her aunt.

"Stop." Caitlyn gripped both her hands firmly. "Sabreena. Breathe."

Pulling in a sharp breath, Reena tried to calm her racing heart, think beyond the irrational panic Caitlyn's words made her feel. "Why are you pushing this now?"

Not that her friend hadn't tried to talk her into getting the children's stories published before. Although she'd never taken Caitlyn's words seriously.

Caitlyn's gaze softened, her mouth curving up in a small smile. "Because you're talented. You should share your work. And I miss the vibrant girl you used to be, the woman who was starting to emerge before Beth had a stroke and died. She wouldn't want you to hide away—"

"I'm not," she protested.

"You are. And it has to stop." Caitlyn squeezed her hands. "It reminds me of that scared little girl I met all those years ago."

Oh. *Oh god.*

Had she closed herself off again? Pulled back into her shell like the frightened eight-year-old she'd once been?

"I'm sorry," she whispered through a constricted throat.

"Don't apologize. I understand. Completely. But like I did back then, I'm not going to let you hide yourself away. Beth would haunt me if I did but that's not why I'm doing this. I miss my friend, Sabreena. She's been slowly disappearing for the last few years and I want her back."

Reena drew in a deep breath. Let it out slowly. Sucked in another. "Okay. I didn't realize..." Nodding, she gave Caitlyn's hands a reassuring squeeze and attempted a smile. "You're right. I'll fix it."

"You don't have to do it alone. I'll be here if you need anything. Remember that."

"I know." Reena's mouth curled into a genuine smile this time. "Thank you."

"So. First up in the Reena-starts-living-again plan." Caitlyn let go of Reena's hands and rubbed her own together. "Contact *the guy*."

"What? No. I can't."

"Why the hell not?"

"I don't have his number."

"Oh." Caitlyn blew out a frustrated breath. A second later she sat up with a grin. "What was his name again? I'll find out not only his phone number but his boot size."

Reena laughed. "I know his boot size and I know where he works. I can call him there."

"Great, do it now." Her friend's brow creased. "Does he work Saturdays?" Caitlyn waved the question away with her hand "Doesn't matter. Call. Leave a message if he's not there."

Should she tell Caitlyn she'd punched the number for the Lodge into her phone so many times this past week without hitting call that she knew it by heart?

No. Best to keep that bit of info to herself.

And as much as she wanted to call Rush, she couldn't. After their last night together, when she'd done something most men would call her a cock tease for, she doubted he'd want to talk to her. He'd probably been glad to see the back of her last week.

"Make the call." Caitlyn crossed her arms, a determined glint in her eyes. "I'm sitting right here until you do."

Spikes of fear stabbed at her belly while flutters of delight swept their way from head to toe at the thought of hearing his voice.

The emotions warred inside her for long moments.

Delight won.

With a trembling hand, Reena pulled her phone out of her bag and dialed the number for Winter Lake Lodge.

CHAPTER 8

In spite of her dragging feet, Reena smiled when she spotted Mrs. Abbott. As she neared her neighbor's gate, she called out, "Nice afternoon for tea on the porch."

"It is. Join me." The older woman waved her arm wildly, urging Reena closer. "Come, come. The pot is still hot and I made scones today. I know they're your favorite."

Reena grinned. Mrs. Abbott had emigrated from England at nineteen. A new bride with an uncertain future ahead of her, she'd held on to her British roots as best she could. Afternoon tea with some home-baked goodness was one of the practices her elderly neighbor had never given up.

Apparently, Mrs. Abbott's mother had an unspoken rule about such things and like clockwork, every afternoon at four, there was tea. On nice days, it was enjoyed out on the front porch.

It would be a cold day in hell when Reena passed up the opportunity to eat Mrs. Abbott's homemade scones. Or anything else she made.

The woman had spent her entire life as a wife and mother, never working outside the home, but Reena was pretty sure you could drop her into the kitchen of any five-star restaurant and she would run rings around the head chef.

In fact, Reena would go so far as to say Mrs. Abbott would give Riley Young a run for her money—and every member of the Collins family plus those who'd had the good fortune to eat at Sunday's were in agreement that Riley was an unrivaled master in the kitchen.

After the disappointment of her failed attempt to contact Rush, the thought of spending some time with Mrs. Abbott lifted Reena's spirits and widened her smile.

Walking up the path toward her neighbor's porch, she said, "Well, if the pot is still hot..."

"Good girl. Sit, sit." Mrs. Abbott poured Reena tea in a delicate china cup decorated with hand-painted roses. Grandmother Abbott's china bestowed on the new Mrs. Abbott on her wedding day. "Now. Tell me about that lovely young man who was here looking for you a bit ago."

"What?" In the process of taking a seat, Reena's ass hung in the air, all movement stopping with Mrs. Abbott's words. "A man?"

"A very handsome one too. I haven't seen him around here before though."

Oblivious to Reena's confusion, Mrs. Abbott continued to serve tea and scones and chat while Reena remained open-mouthed and motionless.

"Quite rugged looking, a smidge of bad boy in him I think, but a gentleman too."

Dropping into her seat, Reena tried to form words, tried to get the questions swirling in her head out. "Mrs. Abbott—"

"Stop that. How often have I told you to call me Mary?"

Shaking her head, Mrs. Abbott pushed the bowls of home-made jam and fresh whipped cream closer to Reena. "He'll be back in a minute, and I want to know all about him before he steals you away."

"Steals me away?"

"Oh my yes. No woman could resist a man who smiles like that when he says her name. He'll have you swept off your feet in no time."

Reena shook her head in an attempt to clear it. With each word, the conversation got more confusing. She had no idea who the guy could be.

She didn't have any male friends who would visit her at home and Mrs. Abbott knew all the Collins men, so it couldn't be one of them...

But who else could it be?

Was her elderly neighbor showing signs of dementia?

"Mrs. Abbott—" At the arched brow, Reena stopped. "Sorry. Mary. Please. Start at the beginning. I don't understand—"

"Oh bother. Time's up. Here he comes."

Reena's head snapped around to look in the direction Mary indicated.

"Oh god." It couldn't be. All that wishful thinking must be making her hallucinate. Her knees shook as she pushed to her feet. "*Rush.*" His name whispered through her lips, through her veins, and left behind a sensation that *did* feel suspiciously like being swept off her feet.

A tug on her arm stopped her when she hadn't realized she'd moved. Glancing over her shoulder, she saw Mrs. Abbott watching her closely, gaze imploring. Unable to decipher what the older woman tried to communicate with her eyes, Reena shook her head and frowned.

"Let him come to you," her neighbor whispered out of the

side of her mouth. "There's nothing wrong with making him work a little for your time."

Nodding, Reena turned back to watch Rush coming closer and closer. Her heartbeat picked up speed and her breathing stuttered with every step he took. His gaze devoured her, the deep blue sweeping over her like the feathery fingers of a lover's caress, and she couldn't stop the shiver that electrified her from neck to knee.

God. This was what he did to her. With one look, he had her fluttering and clenching, dampening in places that had no firsthand knowledge of what they eagerly prepared for, only that he could deliver it.

"Reena." Smile sparking in his eyes, along with a healthy dose of lust, Rush bounded up the two stairs of Mrs. Abbott's porch and pulled her into his arms. Burying his face in the crook of her neck, he breathed deep and murmured, "God, I missed this. Missed you," against her skin.

Eyelids drifting shut, Reena lowered her head to rest it on his shoulder. "Rush." His name sighed from her mouth, her body melting into his embrace with a familiarity that spoke of more than the short time they'd known each other.

The gentle clearing of a throat had them breaking apart.

Stepping back, Reena turned to her neighbor to find the woman regarding her with a knowing smile. "Mrs.—" Reena stopped at the waggle of a finger and shake of a head. "Sorry. Mary. This is my friend Rush. Rush Whelan, this is Mary Abbott, my neighbor."

"We met earlier without an official introduction but it's lovely to meet you again, Rush." Mary indicated the seat next to the one Reena had been in moments ago. "Won't you join us? We're having tea and scones."

Rush's eyes met Reena's, his gaze questioning, when she

answered with a small tip of her head, he returned his gaze to Mary and smiled. "Thank you, Mary. I'd love to join you."

With a hand on her elbow, Rush urged Reena back into her seat before taking the one Mary offered.

Too stunned by his presence to speak, she watched as another cup of tea was poured and a plate of scones passed over.

Rush undoubtedly complimented Mary on the scones, although Reena couldn't be sure. The only thing registering in her ears was the pounding of her heart and the rasp of her breath as it flowed in and out of her nose in short little bursts.

She didn't remember drinking her tea or eating the scone she'd been given before Rush's arrival, but when she finally dragged her eyes off the man beside her and glanced down, Reena found both plate and cup empty.

"Well, it was lovely to have company for tea today, but I must be getting inside now. Things to do, you know."

Mary winked at Reena as she gathered empty dishes and stacked them on a silver tray.

Rush stood and tried to take the tray from Mary's hands. "Let me carry that for you."

"Nonsense. Get on with both of you now."

Without another word, and with a skill even Reena's years of waitressing couldn't beat, Mary maneuvered herself and the loaded tray into her house and closed the door behind her, leaving them alone on the porch.

"I..." Reena licked her lips and swallowed as she turned to face Rush.

He was watching her with that deep blue gaze, the one that sent shivers down her spine and curled her toes. She was helpless to prevent her body from reacting to him.

Her skin flushed, her muscles tightened, and a throbbing beat echoed along every nerve ending.

She wanted to wrap herself around him.

Wished she hadn't stopped him from taking her virginity.

God, she wanted to beg him to take it now.

Instead the words that blurted out of her mouth were, "What are you doing here?"

CHAPTER 9

RUSH COULDN'T TAKE his eyes off the woman in front of him. He didn't know how he'd managed to be polite to her neighbor. Reena seemed more gorgeous than he remembered and had his mind clouded with lust. The only thing clear in his hormone-addled brain was his need to touch her.

"Rush?"

Right. She'd asked him a question. "Vacation."

"Vacation?" Her eyebrows shot up, disappearing beneath her bangs. "Here?"

He grinned. "Yep. You told me so much about Baltimore I had to come see it for myself."

"Really?" she asked, disbelief clear in her voice.

Unable to resist the need to touch her any longer, he reached for her hand. He took it as a good sign she didn't pull away, instead weaving her fingers through his and holding on. "I thought maybe you'd be interested in showing me around."

"Oh. Of course. Where are you staying?"

"I haven't booked anywhere yet. I only got to town an

hour ago, so I haven't had a chance. Was hoping you'd recommend a place."

"You could stay with me." Her cheeks flushed pink and her eyes darted away from his. "I mean. I have a couple of spare rooms."

Smiling, he tugged on her hand until she moved closer, until her breasts were an inch from his chest.

All he needed to do was take an extra deep breath and they'd touch. The thought had his blood racing, his body tightening with need.

In spite of the desire urging him to move closer, he held still, waited for her gaze to connect with his again before saying, "I'd like that. I'd like that very much."

Her lips parted on a gush of air before turning up into a shy smile. "Okay. Good."

Fuck. He needed to kiss her. It had been days since he'd tasted her.

"Reena." With his gaze glued to her sweet mouth, he didn't miss the nervous flick of her tongue on the gentle curve of her plump bottom lip. He groaned as need zapped through him.

She leaned in. "Yes?"

"I'm going to kiss you hello now."

Rush didn't give her time to protest or think about what he'd said before he pressed his mouth to hers. If she was against the idea, she'd push him away, but he had every confidence she wanted this as much as he did.

Increasing the pressure, he moved his lips over hers, nipping and brushing. The sexy little sigh that left her throat and coated his mouth with warmth had Rush's control slipping, his cock thickening and lengthening in his jeans.

That tiny bit of constriction, the discomfort of his hardening flesh being caught inside unforgiving denim, was enough to keep him from diving deep. Stopped him from thrusting his tongue between her teeth and fucking her mouth the way his body urged him to.

With regret, he pulled back and waited for her eyes to flutter open. A shudder wracked him when she sank her teeth into her glistening bottom lip and worried the flesh back and forth. Using his free hand, Rush stroked his thumb down that abused lip and pulled it free.

"If you keep doing that, I won't be able to control myself. I'd hate for Mary to get the wrong idea." Or more importantly, he'd hate for Reena's elderly neighbor to know exactly what he planned to do to the innocent woman in front of him. "Take me home, Reena."

"Home? *Oh*. Yes. Right. This way." She spun around, kept her hand in his, and led him to the street.

He'd had time to think on the drive to Baltimore—over seven hours of time—and one thing that kept popping up in his mind was something that should have been obvious from the beginning.

Reena was a virgin.

And if by some miracle he'd gotten that conclusion completely wrong, Rush figured he was so close to the mark she could count the number of times she'd had sex on one hand.

Unlike him. He'd run out of digits—fingers and toes—before he'd turned sixteen.

He shouldn't be here. Should leave her alone and find someone who understood the rules of no-strings sex.

Except that argument hadn't stopped him from packing a bag and driving five hundred miles to Baltimore.

No matter how much of a bastard being with her made him, he wouldn't—couldn't—walk away.

CHAPTER 10

REENA'S HAND shook as she attempted to get the key in her front door.

Rush was here.

God, he was *here*.

In Baltimore.

At her house.

He was going to *stay* at her house.

The key slipped along her damp palm and elephants stampeded in her chest. It was a miracle she managed to unlock the door and step inside without dropping the keys or tripping over the threshold.

"You have a choice of two rooms. One faces the street, the other overlooks the backyard." Her words quivered and in an effort to mask her nervousness, Reena rambled as she led the way into the house. "The street view isn't as nice as the yard one in my opinion, but the front room is bigger and has its own bathroom. The back room has a shared bathroom, I'm afraid. Not good if you want privacy."

"Oh. You have other guests?"

57

"What?" Glancing over her shoulder, she saw Rush grinning at her from the doorway, and frowned. "No, it's just me."

"And me."

Reena's skin prickled. "Y-yes. And you."

"You and me."

Reena nodded. "Yep. Just us. No one else." Oh god, they were going to be alone in her house for days. Heat washed over her. Muscles clenched and her body trembled with an unmistakable shudder of lust. Her breath stuttered and her voice wobbled when she said, "Which room—"

"Why don't we go out?"

"Out?" Reena stood in the foyer, a little confused by Rush's question and his failure to move more than a foot inside her house. "But we just got here."

His mouth tipped up on one side in that lopsided smirk she loved, making her tummy dip.

Was it bad that all she could think about was kissing that mouth?

"I know but I'm hungry."

Hadn't he just eaten at Mary's?

"Mary's delicious scones reminded me how empty my stomach is. I've spent hours on the road and other than a pack of gum, a bag of chips, and a gallon of soda, I haven't had anything substantial in my belly since last night."

Unable to pull her gaze away from his mouth, Reena watched his lips move with each word and shivered with the flash of memory of that sexy mouth on hers. She licked her own lips while heat zipped through her, tightened her core, and filled her face.

Great, she probably looked like a human beetroot. Not a good look when you planned to seduce a man.

Wait. His words finally penetrated her scandalous thoughts.

"Last night?" She hadn't bothered to ask how he'd gotten here. It never occurred to her that he would drive hundreds of miles.

When she'd visited the lodge nestled deep in the Adirondack Mountains, she'd flown to Albany then rented a car to travel the final distance. That road trip had taken three hours. The lodge to Baltimore had to be half a day's drive at least.

"You drove all night?"

"No. I *am* guilty of not having breakfast before starting out though." He shrugged. "I was in a bit of a hurry."

"Oh." Had he been anxious to get here?

"Wanted to make the most of the six days I have off."

Was it Baltimore or her he wanted to make the most of in that time? Reena hoped it was the latter.

"I could cook..." She tried to recall what she had on hand. Working at Sunday's meant it was easy to grab a meal before heading home so she usually didn't have much in her cupboards or refrigerator, and she hadn't shopped since returning from her holiday. Plus, she wasn't the best in the kitchen. It was safer to let someone else do the cooking.

"Take me to your favorite place to eat. Count it as our first tour of Baltimore."

"Are you sure you want to go out after the long drive?" Wasn't he tired?

Nodding, he said, "Yep. I can't wait to get to know your city."

Reena smiled. "I know the perfect place."

They'd go to Pat's Pub. Maybe eat at Sunday's, depending on the number of customers already there. Saturday night was popular with the locals, and it wasn't unheard of to have a line outside or a bar full of people waiting to be seated.

"Let's go then." Holding out his hand, he waited by the door.

"Don't you want to get settled first? Freshen up or—" The rumble of Rush's stomach echoed off the walls and Reena laughed. "Okay, I get the message, food first."

Slipping her hand in his, she let him lead her outside. Their fingers wove together seamlessly, as though they'd been doing it for years, not weeks. It felt so natural, so right, contentment settled over her.

For the first time in seven days, the itching, twitching part of her stilled. Reena marveled at the power this man had over her emotions.

Two weeks. They'd only spent two weeks together and it seemed like an eternity. As though she'd known him her whole life.

"You're quiet. What's that brain thinking about now?"

Reena smiled. Rush had spent their days together pulling her out of her thoughts. He'd told her she spent too much time inside her head and needed to get out of there and appreciate the world around her. Of course, he'd also said he was the perfect man to help her enjoy it.

"I'm thinking about you."

He glanced down at her with one eyebrow cocked. "Me?"

"Yes. You."

"What about me?" He squeezed her hand and tugged her closer. "Having second thoughts?"

"No. I want you here." And she did. She wanted him here so much it scared her. There hadn't been a minute over the last seven days when she hadn't thought about him, hadn't wanted to be with him. Resting her head on his shoulder she said, "I missed you."

"Good. But I missed you more." Rush slipped his hand from hers and wrapped his arm around her. "Kinda scary how much I missed you."

It was nice to hear he had some trepidation about what

was between them. She needed him to be with her in this instant connection. "It's a little crazy how we clicked."

"Crazy doesn't mean it's bad."

"Didn't say it was bad. And I meant the speed with which I felt connected to you. I've never had that with anyone before."

"Me either." He gave her a squeeze and kissed the top of her head. "Okay, which way? Are we walking or driving?"

"Walking. Pat's is only a few blocks away."

"The place where you work?"

Reena loved that he remembered. "Yes. Well, Pat's is the pub side. I work in Sunday's Side, the restaurant." She slid her arm around his waist and urged him to the right. "Five minutes, ten if we dawdle."

"After a day spent sitting on my ass in my truck, I could do with a dawdle."

"You really drove all the way here?" The thought boggled her mind. It also gave her a thrill. A man had driven hours to see her. Reena couldn't remember anyone driving an hour to get to her, never mind all day.

"Probably should have thought it through a little better, maybe chosen a quicker form of transport. Spur-of-the-moment decisions don't lend themselves to much thought."

"When did you decide to come here?" The idea that he would upend his life to come see her made her happy. On the other hand, if he hadn't thought of it before now...

"This morning when the boss gave me the week off."

"Oh." Disappointment lanced her.

"Hey." He stopped and swung her around into his arms. Cradling her against his chest, he tipped her face up with a finger under her chin and said, "I would have been here sooner if I'd had the time off. I've spent the week regretting not getting your number—"

"How'd you know where I live?"

Rush rolled his lips into his mouth, his gaze shuttering as a light flush colored his cheeks. "Hm..."

"I didn't give you my number...well I did, but you wouldn't have gotten it because you were already on your way here—"

"You gave me your number?"

"I called the Lodge this afternoon. Left a message for you. They said you weren't there. The woman didn't know where you were or when you'd be in but took the message anyway."

He grinned. "You called me?"

"Ah, yes, I, um..." Heat filled her face. "Didn't want to leave things the way we did."

"The only thing wrong with the way we left things was I didn't have your number."

"So how did you know where to find me?" She had a feeling his answer would give her another thrill. Especially if it was the way she thought he'd gotten her address.

Rush sighed. "Could we not worry about that? Maybe pretend I got that message with your phone number..."

"As the bar manager, are you supposed to access the reservation system and the guests' personal information?"

He closed his eyes and lowered his forehead to rest against hers. "No."

"So you broke the rules to find me. Probably jeopardized your job doing it."

"Yes. Maybe."

She smiled. "Thank you."

His eyes opened, their gazes connecting. "Thank you?"

"Yes. Thank you for wanting to find me so much you would risk being fired."

CHAPTER 11

His job hadn't entered his mind once he'd decided to come to Baltimore. "I didn't think about it. The only thing that concerned me was finding you."

Her eyes lit up along with her smile. "No one's ever broken the law for me."

"I'm not sure I broke any laws... Unless you count the speed limits between here and home." He grinned. "I might have bent those a little."

Reena's smile grew and he pulled her into a hug. He loved seeing her happy. She hadn't looked that way the last time he'd seen her.

The memory of her frown as she'd driven away had haunted him all week. Now he was here and she was smiling that sweet, sexy smile he'd spent two weeks soaking up, and he didn't want to ever see her sad again.

He let her go and stepped back, but not before he made certain he secured her hand in his. "Come on. I want to see this Pat's you've told me so much about."

"It's great. Pat Collins and his wife Sunday opened it when

they moved here from Ireland. They had seven kids, who have all worked in either the pub or the restaurant at some point. Some still do. It's a family business, and no one who comes through the doors is a stranger. Everyone is treated like family."

Rush could hear the affection in her voice. Would be able to tell even if she hadn't talked about the Collins family during their time together, Reena considered them *her* family. If what she'd told him was true, and why would she lie, then they *were* her family. The one her great-aunt had introduced her to.

He hated to think of Reena having no one, and while the Collins clan weren't blood related, he had no doubt they took care of her. He was looking forward to meeting them. Expected to get the third degree from some of the male members. Probably the female ones too.

Smiling, he relished the thought of proving himself worthy of her.

He'd come close to proving he was a douchebag at her house. He couldn't go more than two steps inside because if he had, he'd have pushed her against the wall and ravaged her. She'd been so sexy in her nervousness.

She'd babbled and trembled and her gaze kept darting away from his.

There was no denying her pleasure at seeing him though. Her skin had gotten a rosy flush, her nipples had hardened beneath her shirt, and her eyes, whenever they caught his, were dilated, her breathing shallow.

She was such an open book with her emotions. Rush had watched them flicker across her face, in her eyes, and known she'd been as flustered and aroused as she'd been the night they'd been in bed together.

He didn't doubt he could have had her on her back

beneath him within seconds of closing the door, which was why he *hadn't* closed it.

He didn't want to move fast. This thing between them had definitely lived up to his name, and he wanted—needed—to take a step back. Slow things down and build on what they'd already formed.

Fuck.

He'd buried his head in the sand.

The woman beside him wasn't like any other he'd been with because she wasn't the fuck-and-leave type.

She was the forever kind.

And he'd followed her home.

CHAPTER 12

REENA WAVED AT PADRAIG, busy behind the bar, as she led Rush through the pub. Every bar stool and booth were taken; however there were a few empty tables at the back of the room. Weaving her way through, she reached the first empty one and slid into a seat. Rush took the chair next to her instead of across and shuffled it close before leaning toward her.

"You're right. This place is great. I feel like I'm in an authentic Irish pub."

She smiled, glad he liked Pat's. She was even happier he sat so close their legs and arms brushed together. "Mr. Collins is proud of his Irish heritage. He and Sunday wanted the place to have all the characteristics of a true Irish pub. They both worked in one before they came to America."

"I've been in a few Irish pubs over the years, and other than the couple I visited during my one trip to Ireland, this is the best one I've come across."

Pride flooded her. She might not be a Collins and this

might not be her place but she felt a connection to it and she was delighted Pat's impressed Rush.

"Hey. I thought you'd gone home." Caitlyn materialized beside her, a huge smile on her face. "And who's this?"

"I thought *you* went home too," Reena said.

"Nope. Mom needed a hand next door and she volunteered me."

"Oh. It's still busy? Do they need me to work?" Reena tried to look through the opening into Sunday's but from this table, the angle wasn't right, and she couldn't see more than a couple of tables. All of them full. "I could do another shift if necessary."

"Nah. It was just some prep work. They've got it under control." Caitlyn nudged her with an elbow. "And don't think I didn't notice you avoided my question." Her friend held out her hand and leaned across the table. "Hi. I'm Caitlyn Wallace."

"Rush." He pushed to his feet and shook Caitlyn's hand. "Rush Whelan."

"Well, well, Mr. Whelan, it's a pleasure to meet you."

Caitlyn's smile and knowing glance had Reena stumbling to divert what would certainly be an inquisition. "We're here for dinner. Any chance we'll get a table next door?"

"Sure. I'll put your name on the list then bring you a drink. On the house, in honor of your special guest."

Reena groaned when Caitlyn added an exaggerated wink to her offer.

Rush remained silent until Caitlyn walked away.

"She's exactly how you described her."

"Really?"

"Oh yeah, to a T." He grinned. "I'm expecting some lawyerly type cross examination to go with the drink."

"Oh god." Reena closed her eyes. "This was a bad idea."

"No, it wasn't. It's perfect. I get to meet the people you're close to and experience the best pub in Baltimore."

"Good to hear you say that, son." Mr. Collins clapped a hand on Rush's shoulder. "Who's your friend, Sabreena?"

"Mr. Collins." Reena lifted out of her seat and reached for the older man's elbow.

"Stay where you are, missy, I don't need help to stand on my own two feet." Mr. Collins pulled out the seat on the other side of Rush and sat down while muttering about young whippersnappers and not being dead.

"Now, Pop Pop, don't go making a fuss because people care about you." Caitlyn appeared with four pints of Guinness expertly balanced on a tray.

"Caitie-bug, caring ain't the same as mollycoddling." Mr. Collins folded his arms and aimed a penetrating stare at Rush. "We've not seen you around here before," he said, the words holding a challenge.

"No. I'm not from around here." Rush's smile showed amusement, which eased Reena's anxiety. "I live in New York."

"The city?" The Collins patriarch reached for one of the pints Caitlyn set on the table.

"No, upstate. A small lakeside town in the Adirondack Mountains to be exact."

"Ah. Isn't that where you went on holiday, Sabreena?" Mr. Collins's gaze moved to Reena. "You bring a stray home with you?"

"Pop Pop, that's not polite," Caitlyn said.

If Reena weren't so freaked out by Mr. Collins's interest, she'd find him referring to Rush as a stray funny. "He didn't come home with me."

"I drove down today. Reena piqued my interest so much

with all she'd told me about Baltimore, this place in particular, that I had to come see it for myself."

"I bet Baltimore isn't the only thing you're interested in seeing," Caitlyn mumbled beside her.

"What was that, Caitie-bug?"

"Nothing, Pop Pop." Caitlyn hid her smile behind her pint glass.

"The name's Rush Whelan." Rush offered a hand. "Pleased to meet you, Mr. Collins. I've heard a lot about you and your pub. All good things, I assure you. I'm even more impressed, now I've seen the place."

"Well now, that's mighty kind of you to say." Mr. Collins's chest puffed out. "I pride myself on having the best Irish Pub outside of Ireland."

"In my experience, you definitely do." Rush picked up his Guinness. "Here's to the luck of the Irish."

Mr. Collins grinned and tapped his glass to Rush's. "We'll be seeing if you've got the luck soon enough."

Reena's gaze darted to Caitlyn's. Silently she pleaded for help, although it quickly became obvious she wouldn't be getting any from her friend. Caitlyn appeared as interested in Rush as Mr. Collins.

She hadn't had a father to interrogate her boyfriends when she'd started dating, not that Reena had done all that much, but if he had been alive, Reena guessed it would have gone something like this.

One of the reasons she felt so attached to the Collins family patriarch was he reminded her of her father. Or how she thought she remembered her father.

She frowned.

It was hard to say what was real memory and what wasn't. For years, she'd admired the fatherly traits all the older Collins men exhibited, and maybe she'd wished enough to make up those same characteristics in her memories of her dad. She'd never know.

The only remaining link to her father was a grumpy old aunt who had turned her back on an eight-year-old orphan while screaming, "Don't darken my door ever again".

"Hey, you okay?" Rush brushed a finger along her jaw to get her attention. "Did we bore you with our pub talk?"

"Oh no, it's fine." She smiled, hoping he'd go back to talking with Mr. Collins.

Rush's brow creased with concern. "Maybe we should go home. You look tired."

Widening her smile, Reena forced false cheer into her voice. "No. I'm fine. Besides, we need to eat and I've got nothing in the house."

"And we all know you and kitchens don't mix well," Caitlyn said.

"Oh?" Rush cocked an eyebrow, the corresponding side of his mouth kicking up in that sexy way of his.

She moved her gaze off his smiling lips and concentrated on the conversation, not the scandalous thoughts those lips inspired. "I'm not much of a cook. Basic things are the limit of my culinary skills."

"Which is why I get to see your pretty face so often. Want me to tell Riley to make your favorite?" Mr. Collins asked as he stood. "I'm heading that way to grab some supper myself."

"You don't have to do that."

"Wait up, Pop Pop." Caitlyn downed the last of her beer. "I think I'll eat with you tonight. I'll get one of the waiters to bring your dinner in here, Reena, that way you won't have to worry about switching tables or waiting. Two of your usual?"

"I—"

"Sounds perfect, Caitlyn. Thank you." Rush held out his

hand for Mr. Collins. "It was a pleasure, sir. Maybe we could chat some more while I'm here visiting Reena."

"Oh, you can bet your britches we will, Rush Whelan. You park your behind on one of those stools at the bar before you leave Baltimore and we'll have ourselves a nice long chat."

"I look forward to it," Rush said with a smile.

Reena wasn't sure if the two of them talking more was a good thing or not.

CHAPTER 13

Rush leaned back, one arm slung across the back of Reena's chair, the other cradling his bulging stomach, and groaned. He had to admit he'd just eaten the best meal of his entire life. And he'd eaten at some five-star places in his time.

"Damn, that was good."

"It always is," Reena said before popping the last bite of Irish stew in her mouth. She closed her eyes and hummed, the sound vibrating low in his belly.

She'd been making sexy little noises throughout dinner, and he wasn't sure how he'd kept his hands off her.

Okay, so he hadn't kept his hands off her completely.

He'd spent a lot of the time brushing against her—his thigh, his arm, his hand, his fingers—they'd all managed to touch her at some point since their food had been set down in front of them. At least he'd kept his mouth off her.

For an innocent, she had an inherent sexuality that got his blood boiling. He expected once they got in bed, she'd be wild. He'd been with enough women to know a natural sensualist when he saw one.

She hadn't discovered the depth of that part of herself yet. Rush couldn't wait to be the man to help her find out how hedonistic she could be.

Maybe that was what had drawn him to Reena so quickly. She'd sat in his bar with a mug of hot cocoa and caressed it in a sensual manner. As though stroking the warm, smooth sides of the mug gave her as much pleasure as the chocolaty liquid she sipped and savored as if it were the most amazing thing she'd ever tasted.

That first night they'd eaten together he'd wanted to lean over the table and do some tasting of his own. And he'd been craving the same ever since.

No doubt about it. He needed to do some serious contemplating this week. He had six days to work out what he wanted, and if Reena wanted the same.

Six days. It didn't seem enough.

He'd had two weeks with her before, and then hadn't lasted one week without her.

Rush had the sinking feeling that driving away next Saturday would be the hardest thing he'd ever done. It would be far more difficult than leaving home at seventeen without a penny to his name—and that had been rough.

No. He already knew where things between them were going. Walking away from Reena wasn't an option. Whatever happened this week, when he hit the road Saturday morning, it wouldn't be the end of them.

He had the next six days to make sure Reena felt the same.

Rush wanted to delay returning to Reena's house for as long as possible because he wasn't sure he'd be able to keep his hands off her.

It was easier while they were at Pat's Pub; with all those eyes on them, he was able to behave in spite of the temptation she presented, but now they were heading home. Where it would be just the two of them.

The biggest thing in his favor to keeping his personal vow of taking things slow might be how exhausted she appeared. He saw it in the way her feet dragged. Felt it in the way she leaned against him as they left the pub and strolled down the street.

Maybe she'd be so tired he could get her into bed without taking their clothes off. He'd be satisfied with having her sleep in his arms.

Holding her close while she was vulnerable would give him something he'd never had with a woman before Reena.

Their last night at the Lodge had taught him something valuable.

True intimacy had nothing to do with getting naked together.

He wanted that with Reena. Wanted to hold her close while she slept. Wanted to sleep beside her. In his mind, it would be the ultimate show of trust.

Tightening his grip around her waist, Rush picked up their pace. He had to think about Reena—what was best for her—not his overzealous libido. "The next street, right?"

"Yes. Fourth house from the corner," she murmured, fatigue pulling on every word.

As they turned onto her street, he asked, "Are you working tomorrow?"

"No."

"Good. We can sleep in before we hit the city."

"Okay."

They reached her front walk. "Keys?"

She fumbled in her bag and pulled out a small key ring, two keys attached, and handed it to him. "It's the red one."

Her keys were color-coded. "What's the blue one for?"

"Blue one?"

Rush held up the key in question.

"Oh. Back door."

He smiled as he switched keys and unlocked the front door. "No car?" he asked, ushering her inside.

Reena shook her head. "Don't need one. I can walk to work and downtown is easily accessed by cab or bus or on foot, if I'm not in a hurry."

And she had nowhere farther she wanted to go. He'd discovered her trip to the mountains was the farthest she'd been since moving to Baltimore. She'd told him a lot of her history, and it didn't take a shrink to figure out she stuck close to home for fear of having it snatched away like it had been when she was a child.

In the two weeks she'd spent at the Lodge, Rush had watched her change. It was slight, but it was there. She'd grown more confident in her adventures. The timid woman who had pushed herself to try new experiences when she'd first arrived hadn't been there when she'd left.

But how bold had she become?

Would she want to continue a relationship with him?

One that would span hundreds of miles—hours of travel?

He had a week to convince her they were worth the effort.

"Let's get you into bed," he said after making sure the door was deadlocked behind them.

Her face tipped up toward him and she grinned sleepily. "Hmm...I like the sound of that."

He laughed. "I do too. C'mon."

Supporting the majority of her weight, he walked down the hall he hoped would lead to her bedroom. Reena stumbled a little. Before she could trip again, Rush lifted her off her feet and swung her up into his arms.

She snuggled into him and took a deep, shuddering breath, her body going lax against him.

"This is nice," she murmured into his neck, her warm breath sending shivers down his spine.

He clenched his jaw and ground his teeth in an attempt to ignore the lust simmering in his veins. Taking care of Reena might cost him his sanity at this rate.

"Ah...this looks like it." He smiled and maneuvered them into the room with the unmade bed and clothes tossed in the corner.

So his Reena wasn't a neat freak. Good to know. Personally, he didn't see the point of making a bed when you were just going to mess it up again. And while he had no intention of messing this one up the way he'd like tonight, he definitely had plans to do so in the future.

After he'd spent the next few days getting under Reena's skin the way she'd gotten under his.

CHAPTER 14

Reena woke sluggishly, the smell of fresh coffee drawing her out of slumber. Stretching her arms over her head, she moaned in pleasure as muscles pulled taut with a satisfying ache.

"Morning, beautiful."

"Argh!" She sprang upright and slapped a hand over her pounding heart. "Crap."

"Sorry, didn't mean to scare you." Rush smiled as he sat on the edge of her bed.

Blinking rapidly, Reena wondered if it were possible she was still asleep, dreaming.

His smile widened. "Thought you might like some caffeine to help you wake up."

Nope. Not a dream. She'd forgotten. How could she forget he was here?

"Thank you," she murmured while wrapping her fingers around the cup he offered. She brought the fragrant brew to her lips and took a generous sip.

Sugared and creamed exactly the way she liked.

"You remember how I have my coffee?" she asked after another energy-boosting gulp. They'd only had it twice in the two weeks she'd spent in Winter Lake.

"Just one of the many things about you I'll never forget." He brushed a finger down her nose and tapped the end. "There's more where that came from. Meet you in the kitchen. I've got breakfast cooking."

"You're cooking?"

He nodded and got to his feet. "Can't spend the morning exploring the city on empty stomachs."

"The city?"

"You promised to be my tour guide. Thought we'd head down to Inner Harbor today. Visit the aquarium, walk the waterfront. Sound good?"

Reena could only nod. The man had spent the night in her house and they hadn't had sex. Well, not that she could remember... "Which room did you take?"

Rush paused in the doorway and grinned. "This one."

He left her bedroom before she could form another question.

He'd slept in here? With her?

Her gaze jerked to the other side of the bed.

Sure enough, there was a distinct indent in the pillow that wasn't hers and the sheet had come untucked on the far side of the bed, the blanket rumpled.

He'd slept with her. *Next* to her.

And she'd been completely oblivious.

She sighed. "Damn." Disappointed and pleased at the same time, she downed the rest of her coffee.

Banging and clattering filtered into the room. It sounded as though Rush was making himself at home in her kitchen. The level of noise meant he was either doing as promised— cooking breakfast—or demolishing the place.

Intrigued, Reena threw back the covers. Finding herself in her usual sleep shorts and shirt, she tried to recall getting into them the night before and couldn't.

Had Rush undressed and dressed her?

It appeared as though she'd missed an awful lot after leaving Pat's last night. And she'd only had one beer.

Her exhaustion must have been greater than she'd thought. The only good thing about her lack of memory was her current rested state.

She hadn't felt this relaxed, this energized, since before she'd left Winter Lake. Smiling, she jumped out of bed and headed for the kitchen and the racket Rush was making.

Stepping through the doorway, she stopped dead in her tracks. "Wow."

"Hey. Wasn't sure if you'd want bacon and eggs or pancakes, so I made both." He grinned.

"I can see that." There were bowls and pans and food everywhere. Well, the food was on plates, so it wasn't *everywhere* everywhere, but there was enough of it to feed an army. "I usually settle for a bowl of cereal," she murmured, her gaze traveling around the room.

"Not today. Today we need all the calories we can consume to make it through 'til lunchtime."

Lunchtime? Lord, if she ate even a plateful of the amazing-smelling food spread out on her kitchen table, she wouldn't eat another bite for a month.

"Sit down. I'll grab you another cup of coffee." Rush filled a clean mug, doctored it to her liking and placed it on the table. "C'mon, food's getting cold."

Reena moved forward in a bit of a daze. She slid into a seat, wondering where to start.

"So what will it be?" He held out a plate of pancakes. "They're blueberry."

"Blueberry pancakes?" Her mouth watered and her stomach rumbled.

Rush smiled sheepishly. "Yeah. I've got a weakness for anything blueberry. Pancakes, muffins, smoothies. Had a blueberry cheesecake once. Damn, that was good. I haven't mastered the art of cheesecake yet but my pancakes are to die for, even if I say so myself."

She nodded and he forked a stack onto her plate. She'd never get through them all but she wasn't about to disappoint him. He'd gone to so much trouble. Her gaze skimmed the countertops, the overloaded sink.

Of yeah, lots of trouble.

"Eat up." He offered her the bottle of syrup.

Shaking her head, Reena picked up her fork and cut a small section of pancake.

The second the light, fluffy, blueberry-flavored fried batter hit her tongue, she knew she was in as much trouble as her kitchen.

There wouldn't be a hope in hell of resisting. She'd be gobbling down every last mouthful. Sugary and somehow creamy, it catered to her sweet tooth with pinpoint accuracy.

Damn. The man could cook.

Swallowing, she grabbed her coffee and took a quick sip. "Are you some sort of kitchen ninja?"

Rush laughed. "No, but I know my way around."

"I can't believe I had all this in here."

"You didn't. I ducked out to the store before you woke up."

"You went out and bought food?"

He shrugged. "I'm going to be here all week. I can't sponge off you the whole time. Thought I'd pick up some essentials."

"This is more than essentials. What else did you buy? And

how much do I owe you?" she asked before scooping up another forkful.

"Nothing. You owe me nothing."

She frowned and swallowed. "I can't let you pay for all this food."

"Sure you can. You're letting me stay here, so I'm saving on accommodations. I thought I'd repay you by supplying some basic food items and cooking all the meals we eat at home."

Reena liked the way he called her place home. Sure, he didn't mean it was *his* home, but it gave her a jolt of satisfaction to hear the word come out of his mouth. It also delivered a burst of longing.

She *wanted* him to think of her house as home.

The thought brought her up short. What was happening here?

Three weeks ago she hadn't known the man existed, and now she wanted him to call her house home?

"Hey. You're thinking too hard again." Rush pointed his fork at her plate. "Eat. Then shower. Then we're out of here for a day of fun."

She forced a smile and shoveled in another mouthful of delicious pancake. Nope. It wouldn't be a hardship to eat the whole plate load.

Chewing slowly, Reena vowed to stop analyzing every second of their time or the connection between them and do what Rush had helped her do during her two-week vacation in the mountains.

She would soak up the world around her and enjoy every moment of it—of him.

CHAPTER 15

REENA BROKE the surface and spat out a mouthful of dirty, salty water. "Oh my god!" Grabbing the bottom of the upturned paddleboat, she glanced around searching for Rush. "Rush!"

"Over here." His wet head popped up on the other side of the plastic hull. "You all right?"

Wiping hair out of her eyes, she glared at him. "Seriously? I'm in Baltimore Harbor, which has God knows what floating in it, and you're asking if I'm all right?"

As if to prove her point, a clump of indeterminate trash bobbed past. Shuddering with revulsion, Reena used one hand to scoop water away from her, making sure her fingers didn't touch the soggy mess.

"Help me tip this thing back over."

A squeal burst from her throat as she spun around, spraying water everywhere. She wiped her face to discover Rush had come around the boat behind her. "Don't do that!"

"Stop panicking. We'll be fine. As soon as we get this right side up, I'll hoist you in."

A thought struck her. Something else could be in the water. Something far more terrifying than unidentified floating objects. "Oh my god. Do you think there are sharks in here?"

He laughed.

Totally not the thing to do when her nerves were jangled and her mind was conjuring up all manner of horrible scenarios with her and a great white shark in the lead roles. "Rush!"

"Sorry. Sorry." He got his mirth under control and said, "No. I doubt there are sharks in here."

"Doubt? *Doubt?*" She glanced around, frantically searching the water's surface for a big gray fin—and spotted a big gray runabout heading right for them at breakneck speed instead. "Oh my God, they're going to hit us!"

Rush pulled her back against his chest. "It's the guy from the hire place. He'll stop before he hits us. He's probably had to do this numerous times."

Rush's reassurances didn't ease her mind. The only thing that would was getting out of this water.

"You folks all right? Nobody got any injuries I should know about?" the crusty old man who'd rented them the paddleboat called over the outboard motor noise.

"I thought you said these things were unsinkable," Reena yelled.

The motor cut out and the old guy leaned over the side of his boat with a wide grin on his weathered face. "Well now, you aren't exactly sunk there, are you? And they're fine as long as you don't crash them into a pylon."

She spun around and glared at Rush. "I told you we shouldn't get that close."

Rush was trying to hold in more laughter, and in spite of

the fear tangling her nerve endings, Reena suddenly saw the funny side of their impromptu swim.

Lowering her head, she hid her smile and muttered, "Idiot."

"Come on." Rush nudged her with his knee beneath the water, causing her to start and squeal. Chuckling, he bumped her again. "Just me. Let go of the boat and take the guy's hand, Reena. He'll haul you up out of the water."

Turning, she found the old guy looking at her with mild concern. "Are you sure you're all right, miss?"

"I'm fine," she grumbled. "A little wet but fine."

Grabbing the man's hand, she kicked her legs to try to assist him. Except all that did was nail Rush in the chest with her heel, because in spite of the old guy's frail appearance, he was as strong as an ox—and she flew up out of the water and into the runabout in less than a second.

"Whoa." She grabbed the side of the boat for balance.

"There's a blanket there you can wrap around you." He indicated a pile of folded blankets and Reena wondered how many rescues he expected to do today.

By the time she'd wrapped a surprisingly warm and soft blanket around her, Rush and the paddleboat guy had tied their upturned vessel to the rear of the runabout.

Stepping back out of the way, she caught her foot in the blanket and wobbled before going down on her ass in the bottom of the boat.

Sighing, she closed her eyes. Today wasn't going to plan at all.

She was soaking wet, would probably have a bruise from one side of her ass to the other, and Rush hadn't given her more than a peck on the cheek all day.

"Hey." Opening her eyes, she found Rush crouched in front of her. "Let's get you on the seat."

He helped her stand and guided her to the bench seat that ran across the back of the boat near the motor. The old guy went back to the controls, the motor fired up, and they were off. Rush's arm around her back was the only thing that stopped her from tipping over and plunging headfirst into the rear compartment of the boat, where the fuel tank, battery, and motor were housed.

"Careful," Rush murmured in her ear. "Wouldn't want you to fall overboard again."

She could hear the laughter in his voice, knew if she turned he'd be grinning at her. Tempted to shove him with her shoulder, she bit the inside of her cheek to distract herself. As much as she'd enjoy watching him fall over, possibly into the water, she wanted to get back on land more.

"I see that mind whirring away there." His arm tightened around her. "I'm not letting go, so anything you're planning will take two."

Rolling her eyes, she elbowed him. "I'm not planning to do anything."

"Ha. Don't believe you."

"I'm not going to *do* anything. Didn't say I wasn't thinking about it." She grinned up at him.

He smiled and lowered his head until their lips were only a breath apart. "I'm thinking *and* doing," he said, before he closed the distance between them and kissed her.

CHAPTER 16

Reena's lips and mouth held a hint of the harbor water she'd swallowed when they both went under. But beneath that, when he swept his tongue deeper into her mouth, he found the taste he remembered. The flavor he hadn't been able to get out of his head since the first time he'd kissed her.

It was fresh and sweet and laced with a hint of the coffee she'd had before they'd decided to take a ride on a paddle-boat. Her tongue stroked his. Tentative then bold, her innocent brushes became more aggressive as their kiss deepened.

She always started out a little reluctant, unsure, and then arousal kicked in and she forgot about being nervous and went after what she wanted. And she wanted him. It was in the meeting of their mouths, the clawing of her fingers in his wet hair, and the way she climbed onto his lap and straddled him.

Losing himself in the pleasure, he gripped her head and held her still while he plundered her mouth.

Hot licks of lust shot through his belly, settled low in his groin, and filled his cock with molten want. He gripped her tighter. Plundered deeper.

"Hey. I'd let you two keep going but this here is a public place and I've got a business to run."

They tore apart. Breathing hard, gazes locked, they stared at each other as the rest of the world came into focus once more. Smiling, Rush eased her off his lap and waited until she was steady on her feet before he stood.

"Thanks for bailing us out." He shook hands with their rescuer.

"All part of the job." The old guy saluted them and went about untying their overturned paddleboat.

"You need help with that?" Rush asked.

"Nah. I've got it."

"Thank you," Reena said. "I had fun before..."

The old guy laughed. "Yeah, going in the drink ain't all that much fun. Not exactly the weather for it either."

As if Mother Nature were listening, a cool breeze blew across their wet bodies and they both shuddered with the chill.

"We should get out of these clothes before we catch our death." Rush held out his hand to Reena. "Let me help you onto the dock."

Grabbing his hand, she said, "If I go in again..."

"Promise you won't. We're done swimming for today."

With Reena safely on the dock, he piled their wet blankets in the bottom of the boat and stepped over the side to join her. She was shivering so hard her teeth were chattering. They'd never make it home without getting sick. He needed an alternate plan.

Turning back to the old guy, he asked, "Is there a souvenir shop somewhere around here?"

"Sure. The aquarium has one."

"Thanks. Hope we didn't cause you too much trouble." Rush frowned as he watched the man flip the paddleboat over with little effort. "Okay. Not too much trouble then," he muttered.

"All good. Gets me out of the office." He grinned at them. "Go on. Get out of this wind. It's picking up. Expect we'll get some rain before long."

Rush glanced up at the sky. The light dusting of clouds from earlier had turned into a dark, churning cover that definitely promised rain. "Right. Thanks again."

He bundled Reena up against his side in an attempt to protect her from the wind and marched them off the dock.

Heading straight for the aquarium, he hoped they'd find more than the usual t-shirt and postcard in the shop.

People gave them a wide berth as they walked along the waterfront. They got some funny looks too but most didn't make eye contact, which meant the walk was quick.

Bustling them inside the aquarium's air-conditioned foyer, Rush scanned the area for the entrance to the obligatory money-trap these places usually had.

Spotting it in the far corner, he urged Reena in that direction. She'd cuddled in against him on the walk over, her shivering increasing with each step, and now the cold air of the foyer slapped at them, making it worse.

There wasn't much of her, so it wouldn't take long for the cold to set in all the way to her bones. He knew all about the cold. Living in the mountains where it wasn't uncommon to get snowed in during winter, he'd built up a resistance; however he wasn't stupid—he knew it didn't take freezing temperatures for a person to get hypothermia.

He needed to get her warm.

"Can I help you?" A woman wearing a shirt with the

aquarium logo on the breast pocket made a beeline for them as they entered the shop.

"Yes. We took an unexpected dip in the harbor and I was hoping you had some pants and shirts we could purchase so we could get out of these wet clothes." He smiled while tucking Reena tighter against his chest.

"Oh, yes, we do. In fact, we have the last of our winter stock on sale right now. This way." The woman—Tina, according to her name tag—led them to the back of the store.

Before Rush could even look, she was pulling things off the display counter and piling them on a chair.

"You're in luck. We've got one pair of men's sweatpants left." Picking up the pile she'd made, she was on the move again. "You can change in the fitting room. I'll get a bag for you to put your wet things into."

"Thank you." He ushered Reena into the first curtained alcove. "Can you manage on your own?"

"Yes-s." She smiled but he could tell it was forced. "I'm f-feeling warmer already."

"We'll get something hot to drink when we're dry," he promised.

Rush made quick work of stripping and redressing. When he came out of the changing room, Tina was back with a plastic bag and he handed over his credit card. "Put it on this, please."

"Certainly. Debit or credit?"

"Credit." He shoved his wet clothes in the bag. "Oh, is there a coffee shop in here?"

"Yes. Right across the foyer."

Rush hadn't taken notice of anything else when they'd entered the building. He'd been focused on his goal. "Thanks."

"That feels so much better." A smiling Reena appeared from behind the curtain.

He looked down, taking in the way the t-shirt, while not tight, hugged her naked breasts and the indent of her waist before flaring out to sit snug across her hips. The sweatpants weren't much better for his control. A little tighter than the top, they skimmed down her long, sleek legs, molding to every curve and ending with her bare feet.

"Where are your shoes?"

"I lost them in the harbor."

"What?" His gaze bounced back up to hers. "Why didn't you say something?" And how hadn't he noticed she was barefoot before now?

She shrugged. "Not much you could do about it. They were only a cheap pair of slip-ons. I'm sure they've got some flip-flops here I can buy."

He was grateful he'd talked her into leaving her handbag and their phones at home. None of those would have survived their dip; his wallet was waterlogged, luckily he'd only had a few dollars in there. "Right. Flip-flops."

Rush grabbed her hand and pulled her behind him.

"Wait. My clothes."

"Oh." Spinning around, he ducked into her changing room and scooped the soggy bundle into the bag with his. "There. Now shoes."

By the time they left the souvenir shop, his credit card had taken a hundred-dollar hit and he was looking forward to a hot, strong coffee. The line in the café was out the door, and if it weren't for their need to warm up, he'd have suggested they forget it and head home instead.

The line might have been long but it moved quickly, and the wait had the bonus of Reena snuggling into his side for warmth.

When they got to the counter, Reena ordered a hot chocolate and he ordered the blackest, strongest coffee they had. The girl behind the register gave him a funny look as she punched in their orders. Who knew what he'd end up with. As long as it was hot and coffee, he didn't care.

It actually turned out okay. Reena sighed in relief as she took her first mouthful and he had to admit what was in his cup was indeed the blackest, strongest coffee he'd ever had.

They didn't talk. Were happy to sit quietly at a table in the far corner watching the customers around them until they'd taken the last sips.

"I think we're done sightseeing for the day."

Rush had to agree with Reena. His hair had gone hard as it dried. He didn't want to think about what was in that water. "Let's go home and take a warm shower."

She smiled at him. A smile that made his insides tighten and all sorts of naughty ideas about that mouth and a hot shower flood his brain.

CHAPTER 17

Reena slid the key in her front door with an army of caterpillars tap-dancing across her nerves. All those teeny-tiny feet tap-tap-tapping away, driving her completely insane with anticipation—trepidation.

Except unlike last time she'd made the decision to sleep with Rush, she wasn't about to let that niggle of fear stop her.

No. She'd already spent a week regretting her cowardice and chastising herself for being a fool. She had no plans to spend the rest of her life doing it.

She *wanted* to have sex with Rush.

She *would* have sex with Rush.

Today.

As soon as they stepped inside, Reena closed the door and made her move.

She'd never been so bold. But then there had never been this driving need to be with a guy before.

That heady rush of desire was part of the reason she'd panicked last time. Not this time.

This time she was going after what she wanted, knowing

she'd be experiencing new things—sensations, emotions—that would blow her mind. After a week of lamenting her lack of courage and the last twenty-four hours with him, she was more than ready to embrace everything.

With Rush.

Now.

Flinging herself at him, she sprang up and wrapped her arms and legs around his body, making him stumble back against the wall. His grunt of surprise filled her mouth as she locked her lips to his.

She dove right in. Thrust her tongue between his lips and teeth in search of the hot, wet slide of his.

The groan could have been his or hers. Reena wasn't sure who made the sound, or which of them was responsible for the moans and sighs that followed as he let her have her way.

He let her lead, didn't surrender to her attempt to dominate the kiss but didn't make demands of his own either.

She'd never been a fan of kissing. Too much tongue or saliva or lack of both, depending on the guy, had led her to believe kisses weren't meant for anything more than signaling whether things could go further or not—like a traffic light, go, slow down, stop.

Rush's kisses were different.

They were mind-numbing, whole-body experiences, and she hadn't been able to get enough of them in the two weeks they'd spent together. And now that she had his mouth on hers again, she wasn't about to waste a second of the toe-curling pleasure.

She rocked her hips, grinding her aching flesh against the ridge beneath his sweatpants. He was big and hard and she wanted him inside her in the worst way. But first, she needed to stop the pulsing ache making her pussy throb.

"Please," Reena spoke into his mouth. "Rush. I need..."

His hands gripped her hips. Fingers digging in, he held her still. His mouth pulled away and his eyes, dark and piercing, connected with hers. "Easy, Reena. Slow down."

"No." She tried to rub against him but his hold tightened and he somehow managed to move his erection away so she was left humping air. "*Rush*."

"Shh." He pressed his lips to hers in a quick peck. "Not like this."

"What?"

"Not in the foyer with your legs around my waist."

She shook her head. "But I thought... You don't want to..." Reena glanced down at the bulge in his pants.

"I do."

"Then—"

"Not here."

Confused, Reena unhooked her ankles and lowered her legs. "Not here?" *Oh*, okay, they'd go to her bedroom. She smiled. "This way." Untangling her arms from around his neck, she turned—only to be spun back around.

"No. Not now, either."

"But you said..." She searched his eyes for some clue as to what he was thinking but came up empty. "I don't understand."

"You're a virgin?" His tone was questioning but she could see he knew the truth.

"Hopefully not for long."

"Fuck." He dragged a hand through his hair, his fingers snagging on the dried clumps. "You have no idea what you're getting. What you're asking for."

"Yes, I do. You. I want you to be my first."

"You shouldn't want that."

"Why not?"

"I'm not good enough for you."

Reena laughed. "Oh, I'm pretty sure you're going to be very, *very* good for me."

"Dammit, Sabreena. I want things from you I've never wanted with anyone else. We're not talking soft and easy missionary here. I want dark, dirty things I never imagined I'd *need*."

"I want the same."

"Bullshit!" Rush stepped closer, put his nose a hairsbreadth from hers, his eyes swirling with carnal heat. "You have no idea what's going through my mind at a thousand miles an hour."

"Tell me." She licked her lips. Held her ground while his dark gaze searched hers.

"Christ." His eyelids lowered, his nostrils flaring as he sucked in a harsh breath. "I want to get inside you. Fuck your virgin pussy and claim it as mine. *Mine*. Then I want to push you to your knees, make you suck me hard again so I can spin you around, shove your face to the floor and drive my cock deep inside that other virgin territory you have between your legs."

Reena swallowed as heat and lust filled her veins, her lower region clenching hard. She throbbed in a way she wouldn't have thought possible if it weren't for the frantic beat pulsing in every cell of her body.

He moved closer, his warm breath ghosting over her trembling lips. "I'll own every part of you. Every delicious inch of you will be branded. By. Me. *Only* me."

A shudder rocketed from head to toe. The images his words conjured were limited by her inexperience, but she didn't need to have firsthand knowledge to know she wanted to let him do all of it.

Leaning in, he spoke against her cheek as he brushed his nose along hers. "Are you scared, Reena?"

She shook her head.

"Fuck." His head lowered, his forehead resting on her shoulder. "You should be. *I* am."

Licking her dry lips, she barely managed to get a word out through her constricted throat. "W-why?"

His head came up and his gaze met hers. "Because after I'm done taking you in every depraved way imaginable, I'll want to do it again. And again. And again, until neither one of us can breathe or remember our names."

All air left her lungs in a whoosh. "O-okay."

CHAPTER 18

FUCK ME.

He was going to hell.

There was no way he could do the right thing. He couldn't walk away from Reena now if his life depended on it.

God help him, he was going to corrupt this woman to within an inch of her life. But first he had to get control. She tempted him like no other and he couldn't think about anything except stripping her bare and following through on everything he'd told her.

They—*he*—needed a distraction until he could get his head together. He couldn't just go at her. She deserved better than him rutting on her like an animal. She deserved to be seduced, for her first time to be memorable, something she wouldn't regret. He'd hate himself if that happened.

That was why he'd been holding back since he'd arrived yesterday.

"I don't want to hurt you." Christ, the *last* thing he wanted was to hurt her, but she'd never taken a cock, and while he wasn't hung like a horse, he was larger than average. He'd have to be sure she was ready. Get her nice and wet, stretch her out with his fingers before—

"I doubt it will hurt."

He barked a laugh. "Of course it will, but we can minimize it." They'd work up to it. He'd get her off with his hands and mouth a few times before he put his cock anywhere near her.

"It doesn't hurt when I use my vibrator."

For a second, everything went blank. White. No sight, no sound, no thought.

Then Reena's words exploded in his head like the boom of a thunderclap. *"Vibrator?"* His voice shuddered like he'd had one switched on high shoved up his ass.

"Yes. I bought one to try. I know it'll be different with a real penis, but I had no trouble taking it all and you don't seem much bigger. I made sure I got a decent-sized one. And I've used it lots of times without any pain."

A strangled sound rattled in his throat. *Fuck.* His balls had tucked up so far, he was choking on them.

"Are you okay?" Her forehead furrowed with concern.

"Where is it?" he growled between clenched teeth.

"Huh?"

"Your vibrator." Christ. He was on fire. Images of Reena fucking herself, pushing some plastic dick up her... *Fuck!* "Where. Is. It?"

She pointed over her shoulder. "In my bedroom."

He grabbed her hand and dragged her down the hall. They reached her room and he struggled to breathe. Jesus fucking Christ, he was about to blow his load and they hadn't removed a stitch of clothing. "Strip. Now," he ordered as he charged over and yanked open a bedside drawer.

"Ah, it's, um, on the other side..."

Rush glanced over his shoulder, found Reena standing just inside the room, her cheeks flushed, her chest rising and falling rapidly, and her fingers fiddling with the hem of her aquarium t-shirt. "Naked. Get naked," he demanded.

He wrenched his own shirt off, tossed it aside, then dove across the bed. Pulling open the top drawer, he spotted his prize and grabbed it. "Ah-ha." He waved the fake cock in the air.

Reena giggled.

"What are you laughing at?" He stalked around the bed. "You're not naked..." He tossed the vibrator on the bed and lunged for her.

With a squeal, she dodged him, but he was faster. Wrapping an arm around her waist, he pulled her against him, his chest plastered to her back, his cock pressed to the curve of her ass, and sank his teeth into the side of her neck. Licked at the abused spot with his tongue.

"Where do you think you're going?" he murmured against her skin, smiling when she shivered and goose bumps broke out beneath his lips.

She moaned, rocked her hips, and pressed her lush ass against his throbbing cock. "N-nowhere."

"Good." He kissed below her ear with an open mouth, teasing her silky skin with his tongue, before whispering, "Because we're going to pop that cherry now."

CHAPTER 19

Reena's senses were on overload, bombarded from every direction.

So many different emotions crashed together—excitement, fear, desperation, relief, pleasure, arousal.

Before meeting Rush, she'd had no idea it was possible to feel so much in one instant. She experienced it all in a breath-stealing flash, and when the fiery-burst of sensation ebbed, one overwhelming emotion remained—need.

Her body ached.

Every inch, every cell, every beat of her heart pulsed with an agonizing throb. She'd never felt more out of control, more chaotic but calm, more *alive*.

There wasn't time to analyze what was happening. No need to worry about why or how or what next. The only thing that mattered was now was living in the moment and letting each new reaction take her under Rush's spell.

"You still have your clothes on," Rush murmured in her ear before tonguing her lobe with a hot swipe. "We need to fix that."

His fingers slipped beneath the hem of her shirt, feathering across her belly in the lightest caress before he pushed the material up her ribs and urged her arms up so he could pull the top over her head.

She drew in a breath when the heat of him pressed along her back. Nothing lay between their upper bodies. For the first time since that night in his room they were skin to skin.

"So beautiful." He leaned over her shoulder and spoke against her cheek, his breath warm as it fluttered across her skin. "I'm going to get rid of these pants then lay you out on the bed so I can look my fill. I didn't get to look before."

The idea of being naked in front of him made her shiver. They'd stripped all the way last time, but when she'd freaked out and told him to stop they'd put their clothes back on, and in that small moment of nakedness, neither of them had really looked. Well, she hadn't. Obviously Rush hadn't either.

"Still with me, Sabreena?" His fingers worked back and forth along the elastic of her pants.

"Yes," she gasped as his hand slid beneath the material.

His fingertips hovered just above her pubic bone, the light caress a wonderfully torturous sensation that had her abdomen quivering. Heat pooled low, muscles clenched, and flesh dampened.

Moaning, "Please," she tilted her hips in an attempt to shift his hand farther down.

"Uh-uh, not yet. I want you laid out before we get to the good stuff." In a maddeningly slow move, Rush swept his fingers back and forth on the trembling skin of her lower belly a couple more times before pulling away.

Reena grabbed his wrist and tried to shove his hand back inside her pants. He broke free of her hold with a chuckle, and, before she knew what was happening, her pants were around her ankles and a sharp crack reverberated through the room.

It took a second for sensation to register, for the source of the sound to make itself known on her flesh. Stinging pain lanced her right butt cheek and a startled cry ripped from her throat.

Heat bloomed, spreading through her bottom and pelvis and settling deep in her pussy with a hard, driving thud.

Trembling, she moaned, *"Oh, god."*

"Hmmm..." Rush palmed the skin burning from his slap. "Did you like that, Reena?"

He'd spanked her? She should be offended, outraged by the violence of such a thing, but she couldn't muster either of those emotions when the hot pulse in her core told her the answer to his question.

Instead of a verbal confirmation, she pressed her ass back into his warm touch and moaned. It was all the invitation he needed to deliver a second blow, this one to her other cheek.

She gasped, arched, pushed her hips back farther, her ass higher, and went with the conflicting sensation of pain and pleasure.

Prepared this time, she took the sting and waited for the heat to burst, the throb to beat deep inside her.

A sultry moan slipped from her throat when the flare of passion exploded in her pussy, arching her back farther and thrusting her breasts out, her nipples hard peaks of puckered flesh.

"Fuck," he growled in her ear, his palm cupping the new hot spot on her ass. "So fucking hot. This virgin body is so ripe for corruption. You want that, don't you, Reena?"

"Please." Her hips rocked, her skin tingled and her core wept. *"Please."*

His hands curled around her waist and held her steady. "Step out," he ordered.

Willing to do anything that got her more of the pleasure he'd bestowed on her so far, she lifted one foot out of her crumpled pants then used the other to kick them aside. Once she was free of the last of her clothes, he let her go and stepped back, taking all that delicious heat away, making her shudder.

She spun around. "*No.*"

"Don't worry. I'm not going anywhere." He stood at the foot of her bed, his eyes blazing, his fists clenched at his sides. "Hop on. In the middle and spread your legs."

Refusing to be embarrassed by her nakedness or the urgency with which she jumped onto the bed, she positioned herself in the center and leaned back against a pillow, spreading her legs wide.

It took her a moment to realize he held her vibrator in his hand. "What—?"

Rush pressed one knee to the mattress between her feet and held out the toy. "I want to watch you fuck yourself. Show me how you do it."

There was no polite request in his tone; it was all command, and the heat burning in his eyes told her how much he wanted to see her pleasure herself.

She wasn't a prude. She might be inexperienced but she read, watched X-rated movies, and hadn't shied away from sex talk when her girlfriends had shared their encounters during high school and college, so she wasn't clueless or repressed.

A little unsure of herself in this type of situation, yes—her last night with Rush proved that—but she knew what she wanted, and that was this man.

So if he wanted to see her *fuck herself* with her vibrator, she wouldn't be self-conscious, she'd show him.

Reaching out, she took the flesh-colored plastic penis from him and brought it down between her legs.

The device was cold against her heated flesh, the contrast sending a shudder straight to her core.

Sliding the vibrator through slick folds, she lubricated the head and shaft and teased herself with the promise of what was to come.

She'd never dallied before. Normally she'd get the vibrator wet with her arousal and push it in. However something made her go slow, made her want to draw out the process of thrusting it inside her body.

Some never-before-tapped sensual part of her wanted to put on a show for Rush.

She circled the bulbous tip on her clit. Pressure built and wetness coated her inner thighs. Switching the vibrate mode to low, she jolted with the spark of pleasure that shot through her. The buzz of desire pulsed along every nerve, tingled her skin, and clenched her inner walls.

Going slow definitely had its perks. Why hadn't she thought to do it this way before?

Watching Rush through hooded eyes, Reena teased them both, ringing her clit and dragging the vibrating shaft between her increasingly wet pussy lips over and over, until they were both breathing hard and she thought she might come without pushing the thing inside.

"Put it in," Rush ordered in a strangled voice as he leaned closer, his gaze glued to the action between her legs. "All the way, then use your fingers on your clit."

Twisting her wrist, she placed the head of the fake penis at her opening and shoved it deep. Gasping and arching, her hips came off the bed and she wished it were Rush's cock plunging into her.

"Play with your clit and fuck that pussy hard," he growled as he shuffled closer, his hand cupping the bulge in his pants.

Shocked to discover he still wore his sweatpants, Reena opened her mouth to tell him to take them off when he lunged forward and wrapped his hand around hers on the base of the vibrator.

"I said fuck yourself hard." He jerked her hand, dragging the vibrator in and out. Hard and fast, he set the pace before he let her take over and palmed his groin again. "Touch your clit," he demanded.

Helpless to do anything but what he commanded, Reena set to work thrusting the shuddering vibrator in and out with one hand while using two fingers of the other to stroke her clitoris in faster and faster circles.

Typically it took a good twenty minutes and some serious concentration to get close to orgasm, but right now, with Rush ordering her around in that gruff, sex-laden voice, with the sting of his slaps still fresh in her mind—on her ass—and the carnal intent visible in his eyes, the ones locked on her pussy, Reena catapulted to the edge of reason and went right over it with his name flying from her throat.

CHAPTER 20

"FUCK." Rush yanked his sweatpants down and shoved them over his hips. "Take it out."

When Reena didn't respond, still caught up in her release, her body thrashing on the bed and hands working to prolong her pleasure, he was left with no choice but to take what he wanted.

Kicking out of his shoes and pants, he got between her legs, grabbed her wrist, pulled the vibrator from her sopping pussy and replaced it with his cock.

Wet heat licked along his length and sank into his balls. He groaned, shuddered with sublime bliss as everything focused on the unbelievably tight flesh wrapped around his cock.

"*Reena.*"

God. He'd gone at her like a rutting animal. First with her vibrator then with his cock. He'd vowed not to hurt her, to take things slowly until she was ready for him, but in the face of the wanton creature she'd become, he'd had little hope of remaining in control.

Her body pulsed around him. Slick walls gripped him in velvet heat, sucking at his engorged shaft and making staying still impossible. "Reena. Are you okay?" he ground out, shaking with the effort to remain still.

"Yes." Her heels dug into the back of his thighs and her hands curled around his shoulders, nails digging in and scoring his skin as she thrust up into him. "Move, dammit."

Grinding his teeth until his jaw ached, Rush held back, his arms trembling where they supported him above her. "Did I hurt you? Am I hurting you?"

"No. You're bigger. Fatter. Longer. But it doesn't hurt in a bad way. Please, Rush. I need." Her pussy fluttered, his dick throbbing with responding need. "Dammit." She thumped a fist on his shoulder. *"Fuck me."*

Rush could only take her at her word. Had to trust she was telling him the truth. He'd never forgive himself if he hurt her but there was no way he couldn't give her what she asked for. What *he* wanted.

With control he couldn't believe he still held, he began thrusting in slow, easy strokes. Dragging his pulsing length out and pushing back in with long, deep drives that had him clenching every muscle and trying not to come.

It didn't help that her walls continued to contract and release as her vibrator-delivered orgasm lingered.

He needed her to come again. Wanted to feel her slick heat gripping him hard. Tilting his hips, he changed the angle of penetration and hit nirvana.

Reena jolted beneath him, a cry of pleasure ripping from her on a gasping breath. He did it again and felt her buck under him.

Her flesh quivered, the wetness surrounding him growing slicker with each plunge.

The sexy moans and whimpers gurgling in her throat told

him she was close, and those pleasure-filled sounds dragged him closer to the edge with her.

They were the same sounds that had sent him diving between her legs when she'd fucked herself with the vibrator.

The memory of her wild abandon added to the reality of experiencing it under him, sent tingling heat straight to his balls.

Fuck. Too close.

He needed Reena with him.

Tipping to the side, he leaned on one arm and reached between them with the other in search of her clit.

A stroke of his finger was all it took to send her soaring with a high-pitched scream.

She clamped down, trapping his cock inside the hottest, tightest pussy he'd ever fucked. Her internal muscles rolled from root to tip in a wave of suctioning bliss that shoved him right into oblivion with her.

CHAPTER 21

PANTING breath filled her ear and Rush's weight pressed her into the bed while her heart pounded in her chest and her pussy squeezed tight around his cock.

Wow. That was...was... *Wow.*

She'd been right. A real cock was entirely different to a plastic one. It was warm for a start. And softer somehow; in spite of being erect—hard—there was give to it.

After a year of using her vibrator with pleasing results, Rush had just blow all satisfaction and expectations right out of the water.

There was no way she was going back to the mediocre orgasms delivered by a fake penis.

"Worth the wait," she mumbled, her mouth dry, her throat constricted. "*So* worth it."

"Huh?" Rush shifted, his pulsing flesh—still buried deep— shifting with him, sending little flutters of pleasure through her lower belly. "I'm crushing you."

She tightened her arms and legs around him. "No, you're not."

"Reena." He tried to pull away but she held on.

"You're not."

She didn't want to let him go yet. Didn't want the wonderful feelings skipping around her body to go away. Not before she'd had time to memorize them. Carve every single one of them into her brain so she never forgot how amazing it was to be fucked by him. Then again, they could just...

"We need to do that again."

Rush chuckled, the laugh rumbling through his chest into hers, rubbing her nipples against his hair-roughened skin and drawing another round of flutters from her core. "Give me a minute," he muttered into her neck with a groan.

"Okay."

He laughed, repeating the nipple action, and another shot of bliss darted through her.

Breathing deep, she took note of the sweet/sour smell of their sex.

She knew her own scent, recognized it, but now it combined with the hot male fragrance she remembered noticing the last night she'd been with Rush.

He smelled of the mountains, cool fresh air with a hint of hops, the faintest trace of the alcohol he served every day.

It reminded her of Pat's Pub.

Was that why she'd felt so at ease with Rush from the moment she'd met him?

Because he reminded her of a place she'd always felt welcome?

He pushed up. "I need to get rid of—" He went rigid above her. "*Fuck.*"

Reena tensed, her body instantly in sync with his. "What's wrong?"

"Fuck. Shit. I'm sorry." He lifted off her, slowly pulled his body from hers, sending shudders of sensation skittering through her, until he hovered over her on his hands and knees. "I didn't use a condom."

"Oh." The thought of protection never crossed her mind.

"I'm clean. I swear. I can grab my phone, pull up the email with my last test results. I had a full workup last month for insurance." He stared at her, his eyes filled with guilt. "Fuck. I can't believe I forgot to protect you."

He sounded appalled by his neglect but he wasn't the only one who was responsible for their carelessness, and Reena hurried to reassure him. "You're not the only one who forgot. And I'd be stupid to not take you up on the offer to check those results. But it's okay. I believe you." She smiled. "And I'm covered. No risk of disease or pregnancy."

"You're on the pill?" His gaze bore into hers.

Nodding, she said, "Yeah, for a few years now."

"Oh, okay." Was that disappointment that flashed through his eyes? "Let me get my phone from my bag."

He jumped off the bed and Reena stared as muscles flexed, skin rippled, and the cock she hadn't really gotten a good look at bobbed between solid hair-dusted thighs.

She licked her lips. No longer erect, Rush was still long and thick, with a large sac hanging below. That pouch of skin swayed as he moved and her hands twitched with the urge to cup him, weigh those orbs on her palm, stroke the crinkled skin with her fingers.

Would he let her explore? She knew most guys wouldn't say no to a blowjob and she wanted to do that too, but she really wanted to get her hands on him and feel what her eyes were admiring.

He cleared his throat and Reena dragged her eyes away from the cock that had started to swell—thicken and lift—before her eyes. Her gaze connected with his sparkling one.

"You can't look at me like that," Rush murmured. "Not

without expecting me to get hard and pound you into the mattress again."

"Okay."

"Christ, woman. You have to stop agreeing to everything I want."

"Why? I want the same thing."

"You have no idea what you want."

Reena frowned. "Yes, I do. I might not have had sex before but I'm not clueless. Just because my practical experience is limited doesn't mean I don't know things."

He crossed his arms over his chest. "And what *things* do you know?"

"Blowjobs. Cunnilingus. Sixty-niner. Bondage. Anal sex."

Rush choked, coughed, his arms dropping to his sides. "Jesus."

She smiled smugly, thrilled she'd shocked him. "So can we do all those things?"

"Holy fucking shit." He dragged a hand down his face. "You're killing me."

Her smile grew when she noticed his cock was now fully erect. "There's one part of you that's definitely interested."

He snorted. "Interested seems such a tame word for what I feel right now."

His words made her study him closer. His whole body appeared taut, from his clenched fists to the corded muscles in his neck to the quiver that vibrated from his head to his toes.

Oh, and that magnificent cock standing tall, ready to play.

"I want to do everything I've heard about. Want you to show me everything I haven't." She crawled on the bed toward him, intent on getting her hands on him. "Tell me what I don't know about."

"What?" His voice sounded as though his throat had been

filled with gravel, and his eyes fired with such heat, she felt the burn in her toes.

"Teach me."

"Teach you?" he choked out.

Now that she thought about it, she couldn't believe the idea hadn't entered her mind before.

Rush could show her all there was to know about sex. He'd already given her pleasure greater than anything she'd conjured up in what turned out to be a pitiful imagination.

He knew what he was doing. He could guide her and teach her and when he left, she'd be grateful for the time they'd spent together because she would have learned something.

Shoving aside the sharp stab of pain that came with the notion of him leaving, she rose to her knees and looked him right in the eyes.

"Yes. Teach me everything there is to know about sex." Reena grinned. "Start by telling me how to suck your cock."

CHAPTER 22

Words and air lodged in his throat as vocal cords tangled up with breath. Never mind going to hell. He was already there. The devil herself knelt before him. Tempting him to paradise.

The only thing missing was an apple, but let's face it, a juicy piece of fruit had nothing on Reena.

She was lush and ripe and all he wanted to do was sink his teeth into her. Among other things. Fingers, tongue, cock, he didn't care what part of him touched her as long as he did.

Just the thought of pushing his dick past those plump red lips had him twitching and leaking pre-come.

He kept his eyes on hers, watched for any sign of fear, and asked, "Are you sure?"

Smiling, she nodded. Her gaze dropped and not even a breath later, her hand wrapped around his shaft and squeezed. "Very sure. I want to know how to make you come in my mouth."

"Fuck." Shuddering, Rush gripped her wrist and held her

hand still. "Goddammit. I didn't come here for this." Well, he had, except it wasn't all he wanted.

"Oh."

The disappointment in her voice had him reaching out and pulling her into his arms. "I want you. Don't doubt that. Jesus, how could you when I'm rock hard two seconds after coming in your pussy?"

"Then...?"

"I want to spend time with you. Like we did in Winter Lake. Like last night, today." God, he wanted so much from this woman. He was in deep.

Way deeper than burying his cock in her, that was for sure.

He'd never met any woman who made him think of more than a night or two. And there certainly hadn't been one on his mind twenty-four seven for weeks.

"We can do both though, right? I'll continue to show you around Baltimore and you'll show me around the bedroom."

She grinned at him and Rush couldn't help but grin back. "Definitely," he agreed.

He'd never gone for the cute, innocent girls; even in his teenage years he'd only been interested in the ones older than him, the ones with experience and confidence in their sexuality.

But Reena, with her innocence and curiosity, tweaked his arousal like no other.

She also tweaked his mind and heart. He hadn't looked too closely at those tugs. Didn't want to examine them in any detail. Not yet.

He'd prefer to take it one day at a time. Enjoy the moments with her before he had to return home and was forced to decide what it was he really wanted from her—where he wanted this to go.

And there he went again, burying his head in the sand.

Rush knew exactly where he wanted this to go.

He just needed to convince Reena she wanted the same.

The logistics of how they'd make it all happen didn't matter.

Not when he'd finally figured out his heart was all in and he wanted her forever.

CHAPTER 23

"LET's have that shower I mentioned earlier."

"Now? Aren't you going to let me...?" Reena glanced down, but her boobs, pressed against Rush's chest, blocked the view she sought. It was an erotic sight though. One she hadn't expected.

"Of course I want you to. I want that mouth all over me, but we're still covered in harbor water and now we've added sweat-sticky sex to the mix. Besides, you can get up to all kinds of fun when you're wet and slippery."

He carried her into the bathroom and placed her feet on the mat. Leaning into the shower, he turned the water on.

Straightening, he said, "Wait right here."

He disappeared into her room but was back in less than a minute, his phone in hand. She arched one eyebrow in question when he held the device out toward her.

"I pulled up my lab results."

Ah. Taking the phone, Reena scanned the report. She didn't need the proof; some part of her knew he'd never lie about this, but she'd be stupid to give up the chance to confirm her instincts.

Finished reading, she placed the phone on the counter and faced him. "Can I suck you off now?"

Rush smiled. "How about we get in the shower and see where things go?"

"Okay, but I'm warning you—I'm not letting you deter me for long." She'd made up her mind. She wanted to explore everything she'd ever read, heard, or seen. And she wanted to do it all now.

"There's no hurry. You need to enjoy the journey. Some-times it's far more fun than the destination."

"That would be the coming part, right? The journey would be the licking and sucking," she asked as she stepped into the shower stall.

Rush made a strangled sound behind her.

She glanced back. "You okay."

"Yep." He nodded and moved in behind her, a strained look on his face.

"Are you sure?"

He ignored her question and picked up the soap. Lath-ering his hands until they were coated in bubbles, he dropped the soap and grinned. "Oops. Can you get that for me?"

She bent over to retrieve the soap—and got something far better for her efforts.

Rush's slippery hands slid up her spine. "Stay like that. Don't move except to spread your legs."

Reena had no idea what he planned. Didn't care when those big hands moved all over her back and ended up on her butt. He cupped her cheeks, his fingers slipping between to tantalize her with what might happen.

"Are you okay like that?" he asked as he shifted his fingertips deeper into the crease between her legs. "I want to make sure I get all of you clean."

Her legs shook when he stroked her folds. "Rush."

"If you need to stand up, tell me, but I really like you in this position, Reena. I can see all of you from here."

His words stoked the fires of passion from a smolder to a burn, and when she glanced between her parted legs to see he'd crouched behind her, that burn became a blaze.

She really wanted to know what he planned. Locking her knees, she hoped she could hold the position long enough to find out. "I'm okay."

"*Perfect*. What you are is perfect." He dropped a kiss on her butt cheek then proceeded to make certain every inch of her was clean.

His hands smoothed over her skin. From her bottom, he went down her legs, was careful to not miss her feet. Then he trailed his fingers lightly up her inner thighs, teasing her with the gentlest of brushes over her sex before moving on to her back.

He seemed to take special care with each bump of her spine, digging into muscles taut with desire, before leaning over her and murmuring in her ear.

"Time to stand up."

Her muscles and bones had gone soft and it took the two of them to get her upright. "I feel so shaky."

"Lean back against the wall." Rush guided her. "We need to get the front of you clean now."

Jesus. She'd be jelly on the floor before he was done. "When is it my turn?" she murmured.

"Soon." He kissed her. Not a quick peck but a tongue-swiping, mouth-sucking mating of lips that had her limbs trembling and her breath stalling. "Hmm...I like you all soft."

Soft? She was giving toasted marshmallows a run for their money. "Rush."

"Shh." He licked the shell of her ear. "I promise I won't let you fall."

She knew he wouldn't. The only place she'd be falling while in his capable hands was off the cliff of ecstasy.

Leaning against the wall, Reena closed her eyes and let him take her on a ride of sweet bliss. His hands and fingers stroked and teased every part of her from shoulders to toes.

He took special care of her breasts. Working them over and over until the peaks were hard knots of pounding need. He left them wanting, moving lower to tease between her legs in the same mind-blowingly frustrating build of pleasure before backing off and moving on.

Her thighs quivered as he ran his hands over them. Her knees shook when he cupped them in his palms, his fingers brushing the backs in a tickling caress. When he stroked down her shins to her feet, he made sure to massage the calves that had already received his tender care. And then he took care of her feet.

Heel, arch, toes, nothing got left out. He probed, stroked, pressed. One foot at a time, Rush spoiled her with his undivided attention.

If he didn't already have a job, Reena would suggest he get one giving foot massages. She'd paid for plenty and never had one this good.

His fingers trailed back up her body before disappearing.

"Hey." She opened her eyes to find him standing in front of her, grinning.

"All clean."

"That's it? You're finished?"

Rush nodded. "I didn't miss anything, did I?"

No, he hadn't. And she was a quivering mess of unfulfilled

sexual need to prove it. Two could play that game. Smiling, she reached for the soap. "My turn."

Rush's smile sent her pulse racing and her tummy dipping. "Have at it," he said, and held his arms out. "I'm all yours."

Oh yes, he was. Every sexy inch of him was hers to play with. Lathering her hands, she pondered where to start. Should she follow his lead or take her own path?

"Whenever you're ready."

"Don't rush me. I need to decide on the best course of action."

"Any action would be good right now," he muttered.

Reena smiled. "Feeling a little frustrated, are you?" She slid a soapy hand down his abdomen, only to stop short of touching his erection. "I'm familiar with the emotion. Not sure I can help you find relief, seeing as how I haven't gotten any yet."

Rush eyed her through narrowed lids. "You ready to play that game?"

"I'm ready for anything you'll give me."

CHAPTER 24

RUSH SUCKED in a breath and clenched his jaw.

The woman was trying to kill him.

She'd stroked every part of him except the bits that wanted her touch the most. He'd never known his nipples were sensitive until Reena had swirled her fingers around them, never getting close enough to deliver a satisfying brush or tweak.

She'd grazed her fingernails on his skin in places that shouldn't send bolts of lust shooting into his balls, but he'd be damned if she didn't know exactly where and how to touch him for maximum effect.

"Reena."

"Hmm...?" One hand slid over his ass, the other up his chest.

"You're killing me." His cock pulsed so hard he thought it would burst.

"Do you need something?" She smiled cheekily up at him as she lowered to her knees, his cock bobbing in front of her face. "Did I miss somewhere?"

"Fuck." He clenched his hands to stop them from reaching out and grabbing her head. Dragging her closer so he could shove her face into his aching groin. "I can't take much more."

He'd been the one to start this, thinking he had it under control. He was the expert, after all.

But fuck him.

Reena might not have experience; however, she made up for it with enthusiasm. That innate sensuality he'd detected had come screaming to the forefront and he'd been on the receiving end of the most sublime, erotic sponge bath minus the sponge he'd ever imagined.

"Is this what you want?"

Wet heat surrounded his cock head and his eyes crossed. She lapped at him with her tongue, sucked at him with her mouth, scraped him with her teeth.

Basically, she ate him alive.

He'd had blowjobs. They were good, got him off. But it kinda didn't matter who controlled the mouth; add a cock to a mouth and a guy was going to come.

Except Reena didn't just give him head. She loved his dick.

From root to tip, she used everything in her arsenal to worship his hard flesh. He wasn't going to last. Nothing he could think about would distract him from the pleasure she gave him.

"Reena." He cupped her head, tangled his fingers in her hair. "I'm going to come."

He thought she'd pull away, didn't expect her to swallow this first time. She had other ideas.

She sucked him deeper, swirled her tongue harder, and massaged his balls, one finger sneaking back to press against his asshole—and he was done.

His hips jerked, his cock jutting in and out of her mouth as he pumped his seed into her throat. She swallowed him down, licked and slurped and sucked until his legs shook and his cock softened.

"Jesus fucking Christ," he spluttered when he finally had control of some faculties. He pulled from her mouth and sank to the floor in front of her. "Reena."

Leaning forward, he slammed his mouth to hers. He could taste himself on her tongue. He'd never kissed a woman after she'd sucked him off. Never wanted to.

But then, Reena was all about never-done-befores.

Breaking the kiss, Rush lay his forehead on hers and tried to catch his breath.

"Good?"

Her question startled a bark of laughter out of him. Didn't she know she'd blown his mind as well as his cock? "The best."

He searched her gaze, saw her pupils dilated, the blue thin rings around their edges. He took in the rest of her. Heaving chest. Taut nipples. Squirming butt.

"Are you horny, Reena? Do you need to come?"

"Please."

"Turn around. Get on your hands and knees facing away from me." Rush was grateful for her large shower. It meant they had room to move. "Lower to your elbows and spread your legs."

She didn't ask questions, didn't protest his commands. Instead she spread herself wide and gave him access to all that juicy flesh between her legs. He got on his back and slid underneath her.

From this position, he could pull her down on his face and eat her out while his hands played with her ass. She'd talked about anal sex. He'd see how she coped with some finger play first.

He pulled her down over his face. "A little lower so I can get at you, baby." Once he had her steady, he went to work on her clit. Rush wanted her deep in the throes of passion before he started introducing back-door action.

Sucking and licking, he had her trembling above him when he brought a hand into the mix. He probed between her slick folds and rimmed her entrance.

Wet and slick, it didn't take long for his hand to be covered in her juices, and he ventured wider with his touch.

She rocked her hips against him and he wrapped an arm around her thigh to keep her still. It also meant he could hold her there if she balked when he played dirty.

Rush took his time. Ventured back to her anus with a few quick passes before going in for a longer stay. She gasped and moaned when he pressed against the puckered ring. But she didn't pull away.

No, she ground her clit on his mouth and rocked as though seeking more. He wasn't about to deny her. Increasing the pressure, he felt the muscle open around the tip of his finger. She moaned again, the noise dark and gravelly with pleasure.

He continued to work her clit with his tongue, shove his thumb into her clenching pussy, and he pushed his finger harder against her ass.

He'd never initiated anyone into anal play before. All his partners had been experienced and he had to remind himself not to go too fast, too hard, in spite of his urge to do so.

He wanted her to enjoy this, didn't want to force her into it, because all he could think about was how tight she'd feel wrapped around his cock.

A shudder racked her. Then her pussy clamped around his thumb like a vise. She moaned deep in her throat and rocked her hips faster. She was so close. With the next thrust of his thumb, swipe of his tongue, her orgasm broke and her ass opened up.

His finger sank all the way in and he held his hand still while she bucked her hips, working herself on his tongue, thumb, and finger. He'd never experienced anything as erotic as Reena fucking herself with her vibrator, but this—this blew that away.

She sobbed above him, her body convulsing as her orgasm burst into new life. Without thought, he added another finger to her ass and felt her jump another level.

She screamed. Ground down on him so hard he couldn't breathe and had to turn his head. She was out of control and, if her keening cries were any indication, loving every second of it.

His balls burned, his spine tingled, and the woman riding his face as though the world would end if she didn't sent pleasure so bright and hot through his groin, he cursed with the electric jolt of it.

He needed to come. Using his free hand to grab his cock, he jerked his length in punishing strokes.

Rush had never witnessed a multiple orgasm like the one Reena was experiencing. She thrashed over him, her pelvis slamming her forward into his face again and again.

He pulled his dick harder as his balls tightened and come shot up his length. It spurted onto his stomach, the hot wads of liquid splattering over his skin.

And Reena was still coming.

Except now, her body was pushing him out, clamping tight in an effort to stop him from invading. He eased his fingers from her ass, his thumb from her pussy and, grabbing her hips, pulled her down his body to cradle her against his chest.

She shuddered in his arms, sobbed into his neck, and he cursed himself a fool for not stopping sooner.

"Reena, baby, are you okay?" He stroked a hand over her hair. Tried to soothe her with his touch and his words. "I'm sorry. We won't do that again."

"No." Her head shook against him.

"Okay. Whatever you want. Anything you want."

"That," she gasped. "I want *that* again."

CHAPTER 25

REENA WALKED into the kitchen with a full tray in her hands and kept her head down. She didn't want to make eye contact with anyone. She was positive they'd be able to tell what she'd spent the last two days doing with Rush.

A fresh wave of heat crashed over her. Skin tingling, muscles clenching, and a throb hard and insistent between her legs.

Stumbling forward, the tray in her hand tilted, plates and glasses sliding—

"Wow. Easy there."

She looked up to find Mrs. Wallace steadying her and the tray. "Sorry. Must have slipped," Reena muttered, doing her best to avoid meeting her boss's eyes.

"Oh, yes. I'm sure that's it. There's no way it has anything to do with the young man at the corner table who can't keep his eyes off you." Mrs. Wallace winked at her when Reena glanced up. "He's a fine one. Pop likes him."

"Ah, yes. Um..."

"Look at you, all stammering and turning a pretty shade of pink. Reena, I'm so happy for you."

Before Reena could process Mrs. Wallace's words, the tray was taken out of her hands and she was engulfed in a warm hug.

They rocked back and forth for a minute before Mrs. Wallace gripped her arms and held her away, the older woman's gaze catching Reena's in a steely grip. "I'm giving you the rest of the day off. Go have lunch with your new man. I've got Yvonne making you both today's special."

"But—"

A hand covered her mouth. "Not a word. Go."

Reena found herself turned around and pushed out of the kitchen.

Protesting always seemed impossible with a Collins. Caitlyn's mom might have changed her name when she married but there was no mistaking the Collins stubbornness. Reena thought it had to be the first thing stamped into their DNA.

It boggled the mind to think anything got done around here with so many stubborn people working together.

Then again, when all that determination got aimed at the same goal, they were a force of nature. Good thing they didn't have designs on world domination.

Peeking over her shoulder, Reena found Mrs. Wallace, arms crossed, one brow arched, staring at her.

Okay, she really wasn't going to convince the woman she didn't need to finish work early. With a sigh, she turned down the hall that led to the small room the staff used to store their things.

She pushed open the door and almost smacked Steve, one of the barmen, in the head with it. Jumping back—and unintentionally taking a second shot at his head—she gasped, "Sorry, sorry."

"No problem." He straightened from tying his shoe. Grinned at her. "You missed."

Reena smiled. She didn't know Steve all that well but what she did know, she liked. He was friendly and funny and the customers loved him. "Even if I was aiming at you, I'd have missed. I'm not very athletic."

Steve chuckled. "Don't think you need to be if you want to bean someone with a door."

Laughing, Reena stepped into the room. "True, true." She pulled off her apron.

"You done already?"

"Yeah. Mrs. Wallace gave me the rest of the day off."

"Lucky you."

"I'm not sure about that." Reena frowned. She'd been all but ordered to eat lunch at Sunday's with Rush. No doubt they'd have lots of eyes on them.

"Make the most of your time off. I'll see you later. I need to get behind the bar before Tris comes looking for me. I'd be getting the boot, not the afternoon off." Steve waved before he disappeared out the door.

Reena grabbed her bag and checked her phone. There were several missed messages. All from Rush.

She smiled as she opened them up. He'd sent a ton of emojis. Kisses, hearts, flowers, a moon and stars and sun, and something that looked like... "Oh my god!"

He'd sent her a penis. Thank god it wasn't a picture of his actual penis.

Laughing, she switched her phone off, dropped it in her bag, and headed out of the staffroom. The man was incorrigible. He knew how to make her laugh, how to help her relax and enjoy herself in a world she hadn't felt a part of for so long.

He made her happy.

And he was going home in three days.

Her mood shifted. It was so easy to forget he didn't live in Baltimore. Being with him, having him in her house, she'd gotten a false sense of comfort. He wasn't hers to keep. He wouldn't stay. He had a life and a job and it was hundreds of miles away from her.

"Hey. You all right?" Rush placed his hands on her shoulders, scrutinizing her intently with concerned blue eyes.

Forcing a smile, she said, "Oh, yes. I've got the rest of the day off."

"That's good but why the frown?"

"Nothing." She tried to move around him except he proved to be as stubborn as a Collins.

"Nope. Not buying it." He tipped her face up with a finger under her chin. "Talk to me. Don't keep whatever it is running around inside that overanalyzing head of yours to yourself."

Reena sighed. "It's Wednesday."

"And?"

"We've only got three days left, and I have to work all but one of them and that's the day you leave, so it doesn't count." She loved her job, except right now she hated it. Hated that it kept her from Rush.

He pulled her close and wrapped his arms around her. "I'm not disappearing from your life when I go home. We'll still see each other."

"How?"

Rush shrugged. "I don't know yet but I promise we'll work it out."

"Hey, you two. I think these are yours."

Reena turned to see Felicity beside them, a plate of the day's special in each hand. Felicity's rolled ankle had turned out to be minor and she was already back at work.

"Oh. Right. I forgot. Lunch." She smiled at Rush. "Hope you're hungry."

"Always hungry for food when it comes out of Sunday's kitchen." He ushered her the few feet to their table and pulled out her chair. "What are we having? It smells delicious."

"Corned beef and cabbage. It's a Collins family favorite," Reena explained as Rush took the seat beside her and Felicity placed their meals in front of them.

They dug in and Reena thought she'd escaped the conversation she didn't want to have. Except Rush hadn't forgotten, and the minute he'd swallowed the last mouthful, he reached for her hand and wove their fingers together.

"We're not a holiday fling. I know it might seem that way, with how we met and now I'm here for only a week, but I promise you we're more than that."

"How can you be sure?" Reena wanted to believe him. She hadn't wished for something this much since those horrible days and months after her parents had died.

"Because spending time with you is worth any separation or distance traveled." He leaned in closer. "I'll work my schedule so I have four days off every second week instead of two a week. I'll drive down or fly. Whatever is faster."

"That sounds like a lot of effort for only a couple of days."

"I'd do it for a couple of minutes." He gripped the back of her head and pressed his forehead to hers. "You're worth it, Reena. What we have is worth it. I can't go back without knowing you want this as much as I do. I need you with me on this."

She swallowed. Her throat tight with fear and hope and desperation so thick, she could taste it.

CHAPTER 26

RUSH WAITED for Reena's reply. The seconds she took searching his eyes squeezed his chest and constricted his throat.

He had no idea what he'd do if she didn't agree to continue seeing him. If she decided it was too much trouble...

He'd quit his job and move here. Money wasn't an issue. Time was.

Except it would all be pointless if she didn't *want* to be with him. His insides coiled, spiraling tighter and tighter until he couldn't suck in a deep enough breath.

She'd taken too long. He couldn't stand another minute of silence. "Don't answer now. We've got three days."

He closed his eyes and pressed his mouth to hers to stop any reply she might make.

He'd convince her. He would. He had to. He couldn't accept anything less.

She cupped his cheek and spoke against his lips. "I don't want this to end but I don't see how we can make it work. We live in different places."

Rush pressed his mouth to hers harder. He didn't want to hear any of that. Not now. Right now, he wanted to spend time with Reena. Jerking away, he held her gaze with his. "Let's not worry about it now. We've got the afternoon free and there's still places I haven't seen that you promised to take me."

Pulling some cash from his wallet, he left more than enough to cover their meals and a decent tip, and got to his feet, tugging Reena up with him.

"Come on. I want to visit the Natty Boh shop."

"Really? It's kind of a joke around here," Reena said as she trailed behind him out of Sunday's.

"I know. Which is why I want to go there." He grinned over his shoulder. "What do you think Mr. Collins would say if I turned up tomorrow wearing a Natty Boh shirt?"

Reena laughed, as he'd hoped she would. "He'd probably break a pint of Guinness over your head. No. Wait. He'd never waste a *real* beer like that."

As they stepped out onto the street, he slipped his arm around her shoulders and tucked her against his side. She was smiling again and the creases in her forehead had vanished. He'd take that. For now. He'd worry about leaving when the time came.

Between now and Saturday morning, Rush planned to spend every second of his time in Baltimore within seeing distance of this woman. He'd do everything in his power to prove to her what they had was worth fighting for.

CHAPTER 27

Rush sat at the bar nursing a beer and watching Reena move between the pub and Sunday's. She smiled at customers, laughed at something her fellow waitress said, and looked like she was happy. But he could see the strain around her eyes, the look of sorrow in them whenever they turned his way.

They were down to a day and a half. After Reena's early finish yesterday, they'd hit downtown Baltimore and wandered for hours with no particular destination in mind. It had been a balmy evening and they had strolled hand in hand, talking and laughing, sometimes not saying a word.

They'd eventually found a pub—not as good as Pat's—with a beer garden to have a meal and a drink.

Then they'd gone home and had some of the hottest sex of his life. Every time with Reena was hot but there had been an edge of violence, a frantic urgency to their fucking Rush had never experienced before. He knew it stemmed from the increasing tension over his departure.

As he lay there listening to Reena's breathing even out, knowing she'd fallen into an exhausted slumber, that same oblivion had eluded him. He'd stared up at the dark ceiling and mapped out the rest of their time together.

He didn't like the way it made him feel as though he was manipulating her but he had to have a plan. Had to be sure every second until he left Baltimore was used to his advantage.

Today had been a lazy stay-in-bed day. He couldn't remember ever spending time in bed with a woman and not having sex. It surprised him how much he enjoyed being snuggled up under the covers watching movies on Netflix with Reena curled into his side. They'd stayed in their warm cocoon until the last second before she had to get ready for work.

He wished they were still hidden away inside her house ignoring the world.

Except she had the dinner shift and Rush knew her well enough to know she'd never call in sick. And Pat's was hopping; they'd have felt it if Reena hadn't come in. Tris, the Collins who ran the bar tonight, had told him they were unusually busy due to the rumor floating around that Sky and Teagan Mitchell were in town. Apparently, that drew in local fans hoping for an impromptu performance.

Rush hadn't made the connection between the Collins family and Sky Mitchell before Tris mention the famous singer—and his equally famous wife, who happened to be Tris's sister. He also noticed the man hadn't confirmed or denied the rumor.

"Want some company while you wait?" Mr. Collins clapped him on the shoulder as he took the stool beside Rush.

He grinned at the older man. "It's your bar."

"That it is."

Tris appeared in front of his father. "Guinness, Pop?"

Mr. Collins tapped the bar top. "Couldn't convince you to make it a Jameson, could I?"

Tris arched an eyebrow, grabbed a pint glass and pulled a Guinness from the tap. Placing the perfectly poured beer in front of his father, he said, "Do I look like I have a death wish? My wife's here tonight, you know." He indicated the back corner of the room with a tip of his chin.

"Damn women," Mr. Collins grumbled. "They're all but measuring me for a coffin. I ain't going nowhere 'til I see all them babies happy and settled like me and my Sunday were. Like you and your siblings are."

Rush had just brought his own beer to his mouth when a boney finger was poked in his face.

"And you."

He glanced at the Collins patriarch, wondering what the hell he had to do with anything.

"You need to make that girly happy. Give her a bunch of babies and that'll get her settled. She needs it. Family. We all do. It's what makes us strong. Gives us a reason to do better. And you two got nothing, so you have to make your own."

Rush stared at the old man.

"Pop. Leave the guy alone." Tris smiled at him apologetically before moving to serve the customer waving from the end of the bar.

"I'm right, ain't I? You got no one." Mr. Collins tapped the wrinkly skin beside his right eye. "I got peepers and they see more than people think. Damn fool kids thinking they know it all," he muttered.

"I..." Rush swallowed. "What gave it away?"

Mr. Collins shrugged. "Who knows? Could be I'm just an old Irishman spouting nonsense."

Rush chuckled. "I doubt that." He took a sip of his beer and pondered the old man's words. "I'm in love with her."

"I see it."

"Can't say she feels the same."

"Oh, I think she does." Mr. Collins glanced over to where Reena was delivering a tray of food to a table at the back of the room. "She's lost a lot that one. Had it taken when she was too young to know how to handle it. Beth helped but the scars run deep. You'll need more than a bit of patience if you want to stick." The man turned perceptive eyes Rush's way. "And you want to stick, right?"

"Yeah. I want to stick."

"Then here's my advice." He clapped Rush on the shoulder. "Your woman is always right, and when she isn't, she is anyway."

"I'm not sure she's mine."

"Oh, mark my words, she is." Mr. Collins smiled. "I know what love looks like, and Sabreena's got the look; you just gotta get past all that hurt and fear. Once you've done that, you'll stick."

Rush did something he hadn't ever done before.

He prayed.

Prayed that an old man's words would come true.

CHAPTER 28

REENA HATED the tension coiling tight in her belly. She had a headache, knew it was because she couldn't stop thinking about Rush leaving in thirty-six hours. She'd promised him—herself—she wouldn't worry about it, and she'd tried—really she had. But he was *leaving*.

"Hey."

She smiled at Caitlyn. "Big crowd tonight."

"Yeah. Someone started a rumor Sky and Teagan were here."

She'd heard the gossip, and if she wasn't so tied in knots over Rush's imminent departure, she might be excited about the possibility.

"They're not." Caitlyn frowned. "We're going to have to give them something though."

"Is Hunter around? Maybe he'd do a few songs," Reena suggested, scanning the crowded bar.

"Maybe." Caitlyn pushed to her toes. "Oh, there's Ailis, she'll know what to do. Gotta go. Catch you later."

Her friend disappeared into the crush and Reena headed

back to Sunday's Side. It was getting late but things didn't appear to be slowing down. If anything, it was busier than when she'd first arrived. That was five hours ago. She was ready to go home. Climb into her bed with Rush.

She needed the reassurance of his arms around her, holding her tight, to prove he hadn't left yet. Her eyes stung and she blinked several times, swallowed down the emotion clogging her throat.

"There you are." Arms slipped around her waist from behind, Rush's warmth and unique mountain scent surrounding her. "I've been looking for you. Needed a cuddle to get me through the next hour."

Reena smiled. Even in the face of all her sadness, Rush made her smile. "Better?"

"No. How much longer?" He turned her in his arms and bent his mouth to her ear. "I want to get you alone so I can strip you naked and kiss you all over."

"Rush." Reena glanced around to be sure no one overheard him.

"Guess I'll have to be satisfied with this for now." He nibbled at her ear, making her giggle. "That's better. I don't like that frowny face you've got going on tonight."

She sighed and leaned into him. "I'm missing you already and you haven't gone yet."

"We'll make it work, Reena." He squeezed her tight. "I promise you."

With everything that she was, she wanted to believe him. Except she thought the distance and time apart would work against them. Establishing a new relationship had enough hurdles without throwing in living in different states and only being together a few days a month.

"I'll quit my job if I have to." Gripping her shoulders,

Rush held her at arm's length. "I've got some money put away. And I'm positive I could get a job easy enough."

"You can't quit your job. You've worked at Winter Lake Lodge for fifteen years." He couldn't be serious. It had to be a line he was throwing out there. They'd barely known each other a month and he wanted to toss his life away as though all those years didn't matter? "No. You can't quit your job."

"It's just a job. I can get another one. You're more important. There's nothing holding me in the mountains. I don't have family there. Or a house."

"No." She shook her head. "No. We'll work it out without you quitting."

"Reena. A little help here," Felicity called out behind her.

"Go. We'll talk later." Rush nudged her into motion. She wanted to argue but they were still slammed and it wasn't fair for her to let Felicity down.

Reluctantly she went back to work. She ended up doing an extra hour before Mrs. Wallace shooed her out the door in spite of the still-packed pub and restaurant. Meeting Rush at the door, she took his hand and they started the walk home in silence.

Reena didn't mind the quiet. There was nothing either of them could say to ease their minds, and right now, she was content to enjoy a late-night walk with her hand in his. There'd been plenty of nights where she'd done this trip alone and would be plenty to come in the future. For now, she'd make the most of having Rush with her.

They didn't speak when they reached her house. Not a word was uttered as they went inside and headed for the bedroom. And when they stripped out of their clothes and climbed into bed, it was to the sound of their pounding hearts and their shallow breaths.

No words were needed to express what they were feeling.

Coming together, they slid slowly into the passion they'd built over the week. When climax came, it was hot and sweet and unlike anything they'd done before.

Safe in Rush's arms, his heart beating beneath her ear, Reena lay draped across his chest and let sleep take her.

CHAPTER 29

REENA RACED out of the staffroom and almost crashed into Caitlyn.

"Whoa. Where's the fire?" her friend asked.

"I'm finished."

"Finished setting the staffroom on fire?"

Reena laughed. "No. Finished work. I'm heading home."

"Ah, that explains the rush." Caitlyn chuckled. "Rushing home to Rush."

"Funny. But yes. He's cooking dinner." She grinned. "I don't want to be late."

"Don't let me hold you up then." Caitlyn held out her arm, signaling she should go first.

"Thanks." Reena moved past then stopped. "Oh, I wanted to thank you for last week and say how wonderful it is to have you for a friend. You changed my life when you came into it and I'll be forever grateful."

Caitlyn smiled and waved her off. "It goes both ways. Now get. You've got a hot man waiting for you."

Reena grinned. Yes, she did. She had a very hot man at her house cooking her dinner. "Catch you later."

She waved over her shoulder as she powerwalked out of the back of Sunday's. Nodding and waving at a few regulars and Mrs. Wallace, she was on the street and dashing home a minute later.

Rush hadn't told her what he'd planned, only that he'd be making them dinner tonight and needed the afternoon to get things ready. It must be some meal. Reena couldn't wait to see what he'd prepared.

She'd had most of the day to think about their situation—her feelings—without his eyes tracking her around the room. He'd decided to stay home instead of accompanying her to work and while she'd missed him terribly, she'd been able to think.

Two things had become clear.

One—she wanted to keep seeing him.

And two—she was ninety-nine percent certain she was falling for him.

Falling so far that she was willing to try this long-distance thing. She'd already spoken to Ewan Collins about matching her shifts to Rush's so that she could see him every second weekend. She wanted to tell Rush her plan at dinner tonight but expected she'd be blurting it out the second she got through the front door. She was so excited she doubted she'd be able to hold it in any longer than that.

God, she'd been tempted to text him the news the minute she'd finished talking to her boss.

By the time she hit her street, she was running. And laughing.

"Hey, I hope all that happiness is for me."

Reena skidded to a stop and turned to see Rush standing

on Mrs. Abbott's porch. "What are you doing there? I thought you were cooking us dinner."

"I am. Just returning something I borrowed earlier." He came down the steps and walked toward her. "I hope you're hungry."

"Yes, but—"

He cut her words off with a kiss.

She was pretty sure they would have stood on the street making out for hours if his phone hadn't started ringing.

He pulled back and held her face in his hands. "I missed you today."

Smiling, she said, "Me too. *You*. I missed you."

"I knew what you meant. Come on. I need to check on dinner." He pulled his phone from his pocket and silenced the alarm before shoving it away again. "How was your day?"

"Good. Oh! I spoke to my boss. He said if you can give me your schedule two weeks in advance, he can work my shifts around you so we can definitely get together every other week."

"What?" Rush stopped walking and stared at her.

Was he not happy she'd worked out how they could still see each other? "I thought..."

With a yank, he pulled her into his arms. "God. God!"

Reena wrapped her arms around his neck. "So... That's a good 'god,' right?"

"Yes. Jesus, yes." He leaned back. "Fuck, woman, you cut me off at the knees."

She frowned. "That doesn't sound good."

"Oh, it's good. Very, very good."

Smiling again, Reena rose to her toes and pressed her mouth to his. "You promised."

"I did. And I meant it. Now give me another kiss then I really need to check on dinner."

Their lips met and, in spite of his need to check dinner, Rush kissed her and kissed her. She loved his kisses. Felt them all the way to her toes and everywhere else too. When he finally let her go, she was breathing hard and a teensy bit dizzy.

"Wow." She blinked up at him. "That was some kiss."

"There's more where that came from." His phone went off again. "But not until after dinner. I've got this whole seduction scene ready to roll and you're not going to distract me from it any longer."

He grabbed her hand and tugged her towards her place. "You're planning to seduce me? Sounds interesting."

"Woman, I plan to pleasure you so much you turn into a puddle of satisfaction and agree to anything I suggest." He grinned at her over his shoulder as he led her into the house. "It's my plan to not only have my wicked way with you, but make it impossible for you to let me go without agreeing to see me again."

"Well, the second part of the plan is already accomplished. You should put one hundred percent of your effort into the first part."

"Right you are." Rush lifted her bag from her shoulder and placed it on the foyer table. He dropped to his knees before her and said, "Up," as he grabbed the heel of her foot.

"What are you doing?"

"Pampering you. You've had a long day on your feet, so I'm taking your shoes off then I'm pointing you to the bathroom, where I will run you a relaxing bubble bath. Once you're settled beneath those warm bubbles, I'll bring you a glass of wine and give you a foot massage." He raised his eyes to meet hers. "That's for starters."

"Is this the seduction thing? Because if so, I'm all in." Reena picked up her foot. "Hurry up."

He cocked an eyebrow but removed her shoe without comment then repeated the action with her other foot. Surging to his feet, he dropped a quick kiss on her mouth before turning her around and swatting her ass. "Get moving."

A shiver stole through her at the less than gentle love tap.

Rush chuckled behind her. "We might have to do more exploring in that area."

If he'd meant it as a threat, it wasn't one. Not even close to one. She wouldn't have believed she'd respond to such a thing but when Rush got all commanding and dominant, she wanted to lay down and offer herself to him completely.

CHAPTER 30

"Oh my god. You didn't need to seduce me with sex in the bath, all you had to do was feed me this." Reena took another spoonful of the blueberry tart he'd made for dessert.

"I'm going to assume it's good." Rush picked up his spoon, ready to sample his own piece.

"Good? This is ambrosia," she said around another mouthful.

By the time he'd taken his second bite, she was lifting another slice out of the pan. Smiling, he leaned back in his chair and watched her.

She slid spoonful after spoonful into her mouth. Every one was an exercise in restraint for him. She closed her mouth around each bite and closed her eyes, moaned and groaned and licked her lips to be sure she hadn't missed a thing. It was a sensual display of indulgence and he was surprised his cock hadn't burst through his pants.

Sex in the bath hadn't dulled his lust for her at all. But then, the bath had been just that. Sex. He'd wanted it to be erotic, passionately sensual, so she thought about nothing except the things he did to her body, the way he made her feel, the pleasure he could give her—would always give her. Wanted her replete with satisfaction when he kicked her over the edge and her climax released all that pent-up tension. He didn't want that now.

Now he wanted to make love. Slowly, with her beneath him looking up with desire-filled eyes. Not for the pleasure he could give her—for him. Desire for *him*.

He wanted to spend the rest of the night worshiping every inch of her until she couldn't do anything but love him.

He'd been hovering on acknowledging what was in his heart for days. Today he'd opened himself up and taken a good hard look.

He was in love with Sabreena Howe.

His life wouldn't be complete without her in it. He accepted it as the blessing it was and moved on to the next step.

Seducing her into loving him.

He didn't think it would be hard. Thought they'd made a connection she couldn't deny already. She wasn't ready to hear the words from him. He knew that. It didn't worry him that he couldn't tell her yet. There'd be time for that. The rest of their lives.

Pushing back his chair, he stood and held out a hand. "Come."

"Where are we going now?" She didn't hesitate to take his hand. Left her third piece of tart half eaten to follow him out of the kitchen.

"Part three of my seduction plan."

"Ooh...there's more?" She moved close.

Her eagerness made him smile, made his heart thud harder, made all the doubts and concerns vanish from his mind, leaving only space for them. "There will always be more."

"I like the sound of that."

So did he.

Once in the bedroom, he positioned her beside the bed. "Don't move." He quickly made his way around, igniting the candles he'd set out earlier.

"Oh," she breathed. "This is lovely."

He walked back to her and gripped the hem of her shirt. "Arms up."

She obeyed, and he whipped the t-shirt over her head, dropping it on the floor behind him, drawing in a sharp breath at the beauty of her in the delicate peach bra. He only took a moment to admire the sexy underwear; he had other things he wanted to appreciate.

"Now this." With a quick snap, he unhooked the clasp at her back then encouraged the straps to slip from her shoulders with the brush of his fingers. The fine lace floated to the floor between their feet.

God, she was gorgeous. He could stare at her for days and not get bored. He'd get horny, but never bored.

"I can't stop looking at you," he murmured.

"I like it when you look. I like it better when you touch though." She chewed on her lip in a nervous action he found extremely erotic and irresistible.

Bending forward, he brushed his lips on hers and whispered, "I want to make love to you."

Her eyelids fluttered, her gaze searching his. When she found whatever she looked for, a shy smile curved her lips against his. "I want that. I want everything with you."

Rush whispered a kiss over her cheek on his way to her ear. "Anything you want, Sabreena. Tell me and it's yours."

She sucked in a breath, her head turning, her gaze finding his. "Rush."

"Shh..." He ran his fingers through her bangs, brushing them out of her eyes, off her face. "Let me love you."

He did it with his hands. With his mouth. He stroked and kissed and loved every inch of exposed skin from her head to her waist. When he slid his hands into the elastic of her shorts, she trembled. Lowering the material over her hips, Rush fell to his knees to start his worship all over again.

By the time her quivering legs gave way, he'd stroked her to an orgasm that rolled over her as soft as a summer breeze.

She gasped when he picked her up. Carefully, he laid her on the bed and kissed her, everything he felt for her bleeding into the soft caress of his mouth on hers. Hooded lids hung over dazed eyes and he could see her desire for him, sweet and lush, overflowing in gentle waves.

Unable to wait any longer to be inside her, Rush shucked his clothes and joined her on the bed, making himself at home between her legs.

Her arms came up to wrap around his neck, tugging him down to her. "Love me, Rush."

Their mouths fused as he joined their bodies in one thrust. He swallowed her gasp, his tongue plunging between her parted lips in the same steady rhythm as his cock surging into her slick heat.

He kept his eyes open, kept them on hers, as he loved her with everything he was. He might not be able to say the words but he could show her with his body, open his soul through his eyes.

Rush gave himself completely, knowing she could reject him. He understood her enough to know he had to lay himself bare if he wanted her to trust him with her heart.

Biting his tongue to keep from saying the words desperate

to be said, he picked up the pace and tilted his hips. She panted and shuddered, her pussy tightening around him as he drove them both toward the peak.

Her climax took them both. It rose up and burst over her, dragging him under the wave of bliss with her. And when he'd spent the last of his seed inside her, he couldn't stop himself from hoping her birth control failed.

He knew it was the wrong thing to want, a manipulative way to forge a permanent connection. Except the thought of Reena carrying his child didn't feel wrong—being with her forever felt right.

More right than anything else in his life ever had.

CHAPTER 31

"Second week in a row I've found you with that frowning face. What's on your mind now?" Caitlyn squeezed into the booth opposite her.

"Jeez. What is this? Caitlyn's confession corner?" Reena laughed but the sound came out rough, edged with hysteria.

"Nothing better than confessing over a shot of Jameson," Caitlyn said as Ailis put a bottle and two shot glasses on the table between them. "Thanks, Ailis."

They stayed quiet while Caitlyn poured and they downed the amber liquid. Reena winced. God, that burned.

Refilling their glasses, her friend waited her out. She'd always been able to do that. Get Reena to spill her secrets just by sitting quietly, ready to listen to whatever crisis had come into Reena's life.

Needing the courage, she knocked back the second shot and shuddered through the burn, settling when the warmth hit her belly. "He asked me to go with him."

"Rush?"

"Yeah." She nodded. "I said no."

"Why the hell would you do that? You're in love with the guy."

Reena's gaze snapped up, collided with the blue eyes of the woman who had been her lifeline through so much in spite of their age gap. In spite of the fact she'd started out as Reena's babysitter, a teenager taking care of a scared, orphaned little girl barely surviving the loss of her parents.

She trusted Caitlyn. More than she trusted herself, it seemed.

Reena thought she loved him. But having never had sex, she'd wondered if those emotions could be put down to the starry-eyed confusion of a virgin giving her heart to the guy who popped her cherry.

Heat flashed through her. God, had he popped it. He'd blown that thing apart with a load of C-4. It had been the single most spectacular thing to ever happen to her. Until he'd done it again and again and again—

"I'm going to assume that flushed look on your face means you've sunk deep into some super-hot memories of how much 'love' went on between the two of you."

Reena glanced at the smirk on Caitlyn's mouth and more heat burned her cheeks. "Sorry."

"Oh, no. Don't be sorry. *Never* be sorry about amazing sex."

"How do you know it was amazing?"

"Other than the flushed face, we've got dilated pupils, short breaths, and a pair of extra-perky boobs." Caitlyn laughed when Reena crossed her arms over said perky.

"Do you really think I'm in love with him?" she asked, apprehension dropping her belly low.

"You don't think you are?"

Reena shrugged. "I don't know. I've never..."

"I get that he's your first, and sometimes girls—women—

get starry-eyed and confuse sex with love, but you're not the type. You're the most levelheaded woman I know. Mature beyond your years and smart. So very, very smart. Love is often blind and stupid, but take it from someone who's been there, you're in love with Rush."

"We only met last month."

"It only takes a second to fall."

"We don't know each other. Not really."

Caitlyn arched one eyebrow.

"Okay. Fine. We know enough about each other. I guess. Maybe." Reena chewed her thumbnail. "But I live here."

"So move."

"I can't—"

Caitlyn held up a hand. "Let's try it this way. How'd it feel when you woke up alone this morning? How do you think you'll feel when you walk into your house tonight—when you finally get up the nerve to go home to your *empty* house?"

God. How did Caitlyn know?

Caitlyn smiled, leaned over, and covered Reena's hand with hers. "Imagine that empty feeling for the rest of your life. Imagine not seeing him every day. Not touching him. Hearing him. Kissing him."

"Oh, God." Reena dropped her forehead to the table. "I'm in love with Rush and I let him leave."

Caitlyn patted her head. "There you go. I'll tell Mom you're quitting."

"What?" Reena snapped upright. "I can't quit."

"Didn't we just have this argument?"

"It wasn't an argument. It's Caitlyn's confession corner, remember." Reena smiled. The emotion welling up inside her was all consuming.

Could she really do this? Uproot her life and move

hundreds of miles away to be with a guy she'd only known a month?

"What will I do about the house?" she murmured.

"Sell it. Rent it out. It's a minor detail."

God. She couldn't believe she was thinking about doing it. "I'll need to—" Her words were cut off by her phone. Glancing down, she saw the silly picture Rush had taken of the two of them down by the harbor lighting up her screen. "Oh." Reena fumbled the device, almost dropping it on the floor before she managed to hit accept and bring it to her ear.

"Hi." Her voice came out a squeak.

"You okay? Did I catch you at a bad time? I thought you were off work now?"

"No. I'm fine. I am. Off work, I mean."

"Are you sure you're all right?"

God, it was good to hear his voice.

Reena closed her eyes and imagined him sitting next to her asking that question. Warmth flowed through her. The heavy feeling she'd had in her chest since yesterday morning eased.

"Sabreena?" Rush snapped in her ear. "Talk to me."

"I miss you," she whispered.

"I miss you more, baby. God. This sucks. I'm on shift in a few minutes and all I want to do is jump in my truck and drive back to you."

Reena smiled. "I have some good news." She glanced over at Caitlyn.

"Tell me it's that you're coming to see me soon."

"It is. How does weekend after next sound?" Could she pack up everything in that time? Probably not, but she could organize some things long distance. Like selling or renting out her house.

Caitlyn leaned over the table and whispered, "I'll help you."

"Is that Caitlyn?" Rush asked. "Are you still at work? I thought you said you were off now."

"I'm still at the pub. Didn't want to go home yet."

"Don't go home. Go to the airport and get the first plane up here."

"As much as I'd love that, I can't...but I'll see you in less than two weeks."

"Tell me when your plane gets into Albany and I'll be there to pick you up."

"Okay. I'll let you know as soon as I confirm the details." She had so many details to sort out.

"I gotta go." Rush sighed. "The next two weeks are going to fucking drag."

"I know."

"Message me when you go to bed. I'll take my break then so I can call and wish you good night."

"I will. And Rush..."

"Yeah?"

"I...ah, can't wait to see you." She'd wanted to tell him she loved him. The words were on the tip of her tongue, except it would be better to wait until she could say it in person. "Bye."

"Bye, Reena. Stay safe."

The call disconnected and she lowered the phone from her ear.

She stared at Caitlyn. "Oh god. Am I really doing this?"

"Yes!" Caitlyn held out Reena's refilled shot glass. "A toast."

Reena took her glass and waited.

"To the wild rush of love." Caitlyn grinned at her creative use of Rush's name.

Reena rolled her eyes, clinked their glasses and threw back

the shot. The whiskey burned, shuddering warmth spreading through her chest as it made its way to her stomach. God. That was number three. She'd have to eat something before she attempted to walk home.

The last thing she needed was to stumble home drunk. Then again, it might not be the alcohol giving her this giddy feeling.

Maybe Caitlyn was right.

Maybe it was the wild rush of love.

CHAPTER 32

Rush signed where Michael, his lawyer, indicated. The man had driven nearly three hours from Saratoga Springs for a forty-minute meeting.

Yep. Forty minutes was all it took to buy a house when you were paying cash.

The real estate agent shuffled around some more paperwork before handing the pile over to Michael, along with the keys to the house.

Jesus. He'd bought a house.

He still wasn't sure what possessed him to do it. The small cabin—if you could call a fifteen-room dwelling "small"—sat on the edge of the water, in the town directly across the lake from the Lodge.

For something that had been vacant for several years, the place wasn't in bad shape. He'd had to pay extra for the building inspector to come out on Wednesday and give him that news, because once Rush had made up his mind he wanted this place, he wanted it yesterday.

So he'd paid through the nose for everything to be pushed through in three days.

For the first time in his life, he'd used his trust fund.

Fuck. He dragged a hand over his head and gripped the back of his neck.

He'd bought a fucking house.

"Well. That's it. I'm heading back, unless you have something else you need me to deal with." Michael, a man in his late fifties who had looked after Rush's interests for the last ten years, held out the keys. "These are yours," he said with a smile. "Enjoy."

"Drive safe. And say hi to Nancy for me."

"Will do. She was sorry she couldn't make the trip today."

"Once I'm moved in..." Rush glanced around the empty space. Fuck. He didn't even have furniture. "I'll get you guys out here for dinner."

"We'll look forward to it. See you later."

Michael and his wife Nancy had taken Rush under their wings the day he'd walked into the man's Saratoga Springs office with the letter from his mother's lawyers, telling him he'd received a multi-million-dollar inheritance. He'd be forever grateful to the two of them, and while they had a business relationship, Rush knew he could also count on them as friends.

He walked over to the sliding doors that opened out onto the huge deck that ran the length of the house and overlooked the lake.

It was a beautiful spot.

Would Reena like it as much as he did?

Would she feel what he felt standing here?

Rush couldn't, and wouldn't, deny he'd bought the place with Reena in mind.

He'd driven past Tuesday afternoon and hadn't gone a quarter of a mile up the road before he'd done a U-turn and come back.

The place had called to him, and when he'd climbed out of his truck and walked around the house and gotten a look at the view...he'd known why.

He loved living on the water, which was why staying in the staff quarters at the Lodge all these years had suited him. But he couldn't continue to live where he worked if he wanted to build a future with Reena. And even if she didn't want to move here, they could keep this place as a holiday retreat.

Hell, he had the money, why not use it on something he'd enjoy? Something he hoped Reena would enjoy.

His phone buzzed and he pulled it out of his pocket to see Cam's name on the screen.

Hitting accept, he brought it to his ear. "Hey, what's up?"

"I know you're not on until tonight and you're busy on the other side of the lake, but—"

"I'm done. It'll take me twenty minutes to get back, though."

"You're not going to ask what I want?"

"Nope. You know what I've got going on. You wouldn't call if you could avoid it." Rush pulled the front door closed behind him, making sure it locked. Not that there was anything in there to steal. "I've got your back, Cam."

"Thank you. The owners want a meeting with department managers as soon as every can be here. You're the only one not here so..."

"I'm heading to my truck now."

"Thanks Rush. I'll see you when you get here."

The call disconnected and Rush climbed into his truck and shoved the phone into its console cradle.

He had twenty minutes of uninterrupted time and—he glanced at his dashboard clock—Reena would be home from work by now.

Smiling, he turned the key and started the engine then called her.

CHAPTER 33

Reena hung up the phone and blew out a breath. "Oh god, that was hard."

"What? Not spilling the beans?" Caitlyn grinned as she placed another pile of clothes into a box.

They were in Reena's bedroom packing.

In the past five days, they'd packed up most of the house. Today was the last of it. Other than her three suitcases, which she'd be taking with her on Sunday morning, everything had been put aside for donating or boxed up for storage.

The storage stuff had gone yesterday. She still couldn't believe how quickly they'd managed to organize things.

Caitlyn had helped. She'd taken charge and delegated some job or other to every member of the Collins family.

Even Mr. Collins had been there helping. Or course, he'd sat in a chair directing the moving guys instead of doing any heavy lifting, but it still meant Reena could be elsewhere getting more of her life rearranged—or upended, depending on how you looked at it.

"I don't know how I haven't told him." She grinned. "I'm so excited. I have to bite my tongue at least ten times when he calls."

"It'll be worth it on Sunday when he sees you," Caitlyn reminded her.

"God, I hope so." Reena bit her lip. "What if he's changed his mind?"

Caitlyn's left eyebrow arched and the look on her face said "did you just take a stupid pill" but she refrained from saying anything.

Reena held up her hands. "Okay, okay, I'm nervous and worried and excited and why is it only Friday?"

"You could try to change your flight. We'll have all of this done within the hour. Nothing for you to do except twiddle your thumbs tomorrow."

"I could…" She'd have to change her car rental too.

What would Rush think when she showed up early?

What would he say when he found out she was staying?

Would he be as happy as she was?

"Call the airline." Caitlyn held out Reena's phone.

She grabbed the phone and went in search of her purse. She'd need her credit card. It would probably cost her to shift her flight if it were possible.

Surprisingly, it only took twenty minutes to change her flight and five to arrange picking up her rental early.

"Well?"

Reena turned to Caitlyn. "I'm on the six o'clock flight."

"Wow. That's early. Might not be worth going to sleep."

She shook her head. "Not six a.m."

"What?"

"Six p.m."

"Oh," Caitlyn said with a frown. "That's only about fourteen hours ahead of the original."

"No. Tonight. Six p.m. *tonight.*"

Caitlyn's eyes rounded. "But that's only four hours from now."

Reena grinned. "I know."

CHAPTER 34

Rush smiled through clenched teeth at the woman across the bar.

She'd been coming on to him and every other male member of staff since she sat down.

He'd cut off her liquor an hour ago and she hadn't taken the hint that perhaps she needed to go to her room.

He hated doing it, but he'd sent a text to Cam two minutes ago.

Normally he'd handle this type of thing himself. Hell, in the past, he might have taken her up on her blatant offer of sex in those first few minutes of acquaintance. Although he'd never messed with women who had tan lines on their wedding fingers and while this woman's was faint, it was there. Plus, it had only taken two glasses of wine for her claws to come out.

He didn't need to be this woman's scratching post.

"Good evening, Mrs. Delacourt." Cam slid onto the stool beside their inebriated guest.

"Mr. Newell." The vulture—and yes, that's what she reminded Rush of, a bird ready to pick a guy's bones clean—

eyed his friend with the same lecherous intent she'd used on every other male within sight. "Let me buy you a drink."

Clicking her fingers at Rush, her previous cajoling tone turned commanding.

"Get this man a shot of the best scotch you have."

Rush raised an eyebrow at Cam.

"That's a lovely gesture, Mrs. Delacourt, but—"

"Call me Veronica, or Roni. My *close* friends call me Roni," she interrupted while attempting to lean in and reveal her obviously surgically enhanced cleavage to Cam.

Unfortunately, she'd really had too much to drink, and she toppled forward, almost landing face-first in Cam's lap.

"Jesus," Cam muttered, his hands on her shoulders to keep her out of his crotch. "Time to get you to bed."

"Yes." The woman smiled up at Cam. "Take me to bed."

Cam glanced over at Rush. "This is not happening."

Rush grinned. "Oh, yes it is, and you, my friend, are the one who has to deal with it."

"Chicken."

Rush laughed. "Yep. Yellow as they come and flapping my wings."

Cam got to his feet and hauled Mrs. Delacourt with him, pinning her to his side to keep her upright. Rush might have cut her off an hour ago but the damage had been done. The woman was pickled.

"I'll be back," Cam said. "And I'll want that scotch."

"Yes, boss." He saluted him.

Cam rolled his eyes, turned away, and stumbled a little before finding his balance. "Make that two," he called as he all but dragged his practically passed-out burden from the bar.

Rush scanned the room. Things had been hopping earlier but it was a slow now. One guy sat in the corner nursing the same bourbon he'd held three hours ago. A couple made out in the other corner, the champagne they'd consumed in celebration of their engagement long gone.

Then there was the group of four women out to forget all about husbands, children, housework. They were regulars and Rush knew them all by name.

By his calculation, Cam would be back in fifteen minutes, enough time for Rush to restock the refrigerators before he poured his boss that drink.

He made a quick mental note of what he needed and headed into the storeroom. He hoisted a case of Blue Moon and grabbed two bottles of champagne—to replace the ones the newly engaged had consumed—and headed back out.

He didn't notice the woman at the end of the bar, didn't look that way until she spoke—and everything inside him stilled.

Sucking air into lungs that had turned into vacuums, Rush placed the two bottles of champagne on the bar and lowered the case to the floor at his feet. Only then did he turn to see if perhaps he'd finally lost his mind.

"*Sabreena*."

She gave him a finger wave and a wobbly smile.

"Reena?" He took a step toward her. "I…"

"Hi." Her smile fell a little. "Um, so, I—"

He vaulted the bar so fast his head spun. Then again, that could be the woman in front of him.

"Reena." She was in his arms, pressed against his chest so tight he was certain she couldn't breathe, but he couldn't let her go. Not yet.

"Rush." Pushing against him, she managed to put some space between them. Laughing, she looked up at him. "I guess that means you *are* happy to see me. That stunned mullet face had me worried for a moment."

"What are you doing here? Not that I'm complaining, but

you aren't supposed to be coming up here until next weekend." Fuck. She was in his arms. He'd missed holding her so much he wasn't sure he'd be able to let go anytime soon.

"There's been a change of plans." She studied him closely. "How would you feel about seeing me more often than every other week?"

"Reena," he lowered his forehead to hers, "I'd be happy to see you every second of my life, but—"

"Okay." She grinned at him. "But I'm not sure your boss would be happy if I came to work with you."

"What?"

"Also, do you think it would be all right if I stayed with you, or should I book a room until I find somewhere else?"

"Find somewhere..." He let her go, but only so he could grab her face in his hands. "What are you talking about?"

"I need somewhere to stay."

"You'll stay with me until you go home."

"Ah, well, about that..." She shrugged. "I discovered something when you left last week. Something I'd never realized—and something that changed everything."

"Okay." She wasn't making sense, and Rush wanted to let her get to whatever it was she was trying to say, he really did, he just couldn't wait another minute to get his mouth on hers. So when she opened her mouth to speak, he took full advantage and kissed her.

Her hands slid up his chest and around his neck, her fingers toying with his hair. He removed his hands from her face and wrapped his arms around her waist, lifting her off her feet. Turning, he planted her ass on the bar and nudged her knees apart to make room for him to move in close.

"Well. I'm not sure what's worse. Being fondled by a drunken guest in an elevator, or finding my bar manager groping a guest on top of said bar."

Rush tore his mouth from Reena's. Breathing hard, he stared into her heavy-lidded eyes and smiled. "You're here."

"I'm here."

He ignored Cam, who'd taken a seat a few stools away. "You're here early, and you need somewhere to stay. Plus, you aren't sure you can give me every second of my life because my boss," he tipped his head in Cam's direction, "wouldn't be happy if I brought you to work with me."

Reena nodded.

"Fuck. What did you do?"

She opened her mouth and he placed a hand over it.

"Wait. Give me a second. Jesus. Shit. Okay. Okay." He sucked in a breath then took his hand away. "Go."

"After you'd gone, I discovered that home isn't a place. Not a house, or a city, or anywhere on earth except here." She pressed her hand to her chest. "Home is where the heart is—and my heart is with you, Rush Whelan. I love you."

Dear God. His knees shook and he had to lock them to remain upright. "Sabreena." He cupped her cheek and she leaned into his touch, turned, and kissed his palm. "Baby."

"So anyway," she said as she straightened. "I quit my job, packed up my house, and put it on the market, and came to where my home is."

"Fuck." His knees gave out. "I need to sit."

Reena laughed when his ass hit the stool hard. "Nice to know I can sweep you off your feet the way you did me."

He rested his forehead on her thigh. "Cam."

"Yeah."

"I need someone to cover the rest of my shift."

"Done." His friend got up and walked around the bar. "I'll see you tomorrow."

"I'll be bringing an assistant." Rush lifted his head and smiled at Reena. "I happen to know she's great at taking orders and serving drinks, so I'll be sure to put her to good use."

"Really? Does she want a job?"

Reena's lips curled up as she looked at Cam. "Are you offering?"

"Yes. I'll have paperwork ready for you when you get here tomorrow."

Rush stood and lifted Reena off the bar. "You want to work at the Lodge?"

She slipped her hand into his and pressed against him. "If it means you get to see me every second of your life, yes."

"You have to stop agreeing to everything I want."

"Why? It's worked out really well for me so far."

She was right, it had. And if she was going to keep doing it... "I want you to live with me."

"I don't think we can live in your room here. It's too small."

He shoved his hand in his pocket and pulled out his keys. "How about a house?"

"A house?"

"I bought a house. For us."

"You bought a house? For us?"

"Yes."

"Here? Near the Lodge?"

"No, it's in a little town around the lake. Broken Bay is straight across the lake from here, actually, but you have to drive around. On a clear day, you can see the Lodge from our deck."

"When did you do this?"

"Today."

"Rush, it takes weeks to buy a house. I should know. I've spent the last week organizing selling mine, and the agent said even if I got an offer straight away, it would be weeks before the new owners took possession."

"Yeah, well, the place hasn't been lived in for a while and you'd be amazed at what you can do with a little bit of money. I told you I had some put away." He inwardly winced at how much he had.

He'd have to tell her about that, but not now. Now he wanted to take her to the place where their hearts were going to build a home.

"Come on. Let me show you."

EPILOGUE

"It's not that cold. We probably don't need a fire." Reena watched the flames dancing in the fireplace of the master bedroom.

Rush's arms tightened around her. "I know. I couldn't resist."

She smiled. "I love the house. It's perfect."

"It needs some work," he murmured.

"What it needs is some TLC." She turned her head to look at him. "I think we have enough love to go around."

"We've got time." He dropped a kiss on her forehead. "First thing we need to do is get a bed. The floor is killing my ass."

Reena laughed. There was nothing in the house. Not a stick of furniture. Oh, and the electricity wasn't on either. They definitely had some work to do. "We could sit on the mattress Cam let you bring over from your room."

"That's all the way over there and I want to sit by the fire with you."

"Then why don't we pull the mattress over here?"

"Don't want to risk any sparks lighting it up."

Rush was right. There was no fireguard and while she didn't think a spark would set the floor on fire, it could definitely scorch it and she hated to think what one would do to a mattress. "We should put the fire out before we go to sleep."

"Are you tired?"

"No." She turned in Rush's arms and crawled onto his lap. "But I want to make love to you, and if this floor is killing your ass, we're not doing it here."

Rush stood, taking her with him. "I'll put it out after we make love. I want to see you in the firelight."

He walked to the bed and set her on her feet. Piece by piece, they removed each other's clothes until the only thing covering them was the flickering glow of orange from the flames across the room.

"You know, I think I got it wrong. That heart and home thing."

"Oh?"

"This house feels like home."

"No. You were right. It only feels that way because we're here. Our love makes this place a home."

If you enjoyed this book, please consider leaving a review. It only takes a few minutes and you'll be helping other readers find stories they'll enjoy, as well as supporting authors you love.

For what's coming next, latest releases, sales and more, join
Rhian's Royal Readers
http://www.rhiancahill.com/contact/newsletter/

ACKNOWLEDGMENTS

I love Winter Lake and these characters and I can't believe we've reached Reena and Rush.

There's so many people who had a hand in this series—the first version of each story and the versions that now find their home in Winter Lake. I'm going to list them but I'm sure I'll miss a few.

Erin, Carly, Mari, Melanie and Shawna without you these characters would probably still be playing around in my head.

Dana, damn girl, these covers are everything I wanted and more. Thank you.

Fedora, what can I say? I swear, I don't understand why you haven't beaten me to death by now.

Tamara, Kristy, Amy, Eileen, Lisa, Paige, Jen, Kim, Isha and Ciara. Thanks for always taking a chance on my books.

Shana your friendship has been a comfort and a motivation. Thank you for being there.

Mr.C your patience and understanding when I say I have to work all weekend or late into the night can never be overlooked.

Thank you to every reader who picked up one of the Winter Lake books. Without you I wouldn't be here, doing what I love.

xoxo

Rhian

ABOUT THE AUTHOR

Rhian Cahill is the alter ego of a former stay-at-home mother of four. With motherly duties rapidly dwindling, Rhian is able to make use of the fertile imagination she used to keep herself sane for all those years of slavery. Years spent living overseas and visiting tropical climates have helped inspire some steamy stories.

Multi-published in erotic romance, paranormal romance, and contemporary romance, Rhian, with the help of Mr. Muse, spends her days and nights writing.

When not glued to the keyboard you'll find her, book or knitting in hand, avoiding any and all housework as much as possible.

For more on Rhian –
Website – http://www.rhiancahill.com/
Newsletter signup – http://www.rhiancahill.com/
contact/newsletter/
FaceBook – https://www.facebook.com/RhianCahillAuthor
Instagram – http://instagram.com/rhiancahill/
Twitter – https://twitter.com/RhianCahill
BookBub – https://www.bookbub.com/authors/rhian-cahill
Goodreads – https://www.goodreads.com/rhian_cahill

Love Me Like You Do

First comes love, then comes marriage, then comes baby…

wait, scratch that. Can we start with the babies?

Selling most of her possessions, breaking her lease and driving across the country in search of a man who might not want to see her probably wasn't such a great idea. Throw in an aging car with no heat, snow covered mountains and a rapidly expanding pregnant belly and Covington Valenti may have made the biggest mistake of her life.

When the woman who's had him twisted up for over a year turns up in Winter Lake Tristan Harding is more than happy to see her. What he's not so sure about is her extra baggage. But Tris is nothing if not a loyal friend and if Cov needs his help she has it—even if that means stepping up for someone else's kid.

Love The Way You Are

Who needs 20/20 vision to find true love?

There's something familiar about the gorgeous woman across the crowded club. When he "accidentally" bumps into her, Alex Dean is shocked to discover what it is. The tall, leggy blonde is none other than Sadie Emerson, his college math tutor—and the subject of more fantasies than he could count. Years later, she's looking better than ever. He has to have her. Tonight.

Does it really matter that she thinks she's going home with his buddy, Alec Dane?

Apparently it does because she sneaks away the morning after. *Twice.* First, when she discovers her mistake, then when she decides her upcoming move to Winter Lake makes them a two-day stand at best. But the sex is off-the-charts combustible, and Alex is already seeing stars, hearing bells...envisioning houses and picket fences and other things he'd never considered.

Now all he has to do is convince Sadie his feelings are real. His shy wallflower might consider him a mistake—but Alex has never been more certain.

When You Love Someone

When it comes to love the tough guys always go down the hardest.

Sophie Collins is used to the adoring attention from her fans but the overzealous one who cooked her a meal and left it—with heating instructions—in her fridge has gone too far. No longer safe in her own house, she hops a plane and travels halfway around the world.

He was sent to bring her home safe. But from the minute Sophie falls into Stone's arms he knows she's not the only thing in danger. He's a hardened warrior trained to kill with his bare hands and one too sweet too young pop singer is bringing him to his knees.

If he can't keep her safe and neutralize the threat he stands to lose more than his client. He'll lose his heart.

Let Me Love You

He's got moves on — and off — the field.

As receiver for the Miami Storm, Grady Murdock couldn't be more satisfied with his professional life. Next up—his personal one. He's a player on the field, not off, so when he claps eyes on Melinda at a Storm event, he's neither surprised nor alarmed to find she triggers both lustful and long-term thoughts. Six years his senior, Mel isn't so easily convinced.

Independent, career-minded Melinda Shaw has singlehandedly built one of Miami's premier event-management companies, but success hasn't stopped her heart from shifting its focus to marriage and children. Still, she's not about to burden a younger man with her fantasies of familial grandeur...until she does.

Their combustible sexual chemistry notwithstanding, Grady still has to work overtime to convince Mel he wants her despite their impending parenthood, not because of it. It'll take almost losing everything—and more than a few of Grady's famous moves—to score Mel's heart once and for all.

Hearts Are Wild Series

No More Talking (novella)

Dare You To (novella)

Mad Love

Boys Of Summer

Bondi Beach Boys

Sand, Surf And Sunnie

Only You Series

All Of You

Holiday Romances

Christmas Wishes

New Year's Kisses

Valentine's Dates

Secret Santa

Frosty's Snowmen Series

A Touch Of Frost

A Kiss From Kringle

A Taste For Kandy

Secret Confessions

Sydney Housewives – Virginia

Standalone Titles

Make You Burn

9 781925 375473